I0618967

Soul Keeper

Boone's Journey

Published by E&H Publishing

Chapter One

"All rise!" The court usher yelled.

The rustling of paper and shuffling feet echoed through the large room. The crowd stood, one after the other, seemingly out of a reverie of boredom. The ticking of a clock that hung above their heads crawled forward as the crowd waited in complete silence until the judge walked into the room and took his throne at the front, towering over his onlookers.

It was cold, in both temperature and temperament. The room, now so silent you could hear a pin drop, was new, having only been built thirty years prior. The ceiling was high, but light shone in through the large glass dome, which covered the middle section of the roof. Devoid of colour, the room remained a neutral ugly brown colour, covering the floors to the tables and chairs and all the way to the walls. Every single inch of the room lacked vitality. The only sign of colour was from the Royal Coat of Arms, just behind where the judge would preside.

A stern, older-looking man entered the room. It was a face that told you he had seen many years of people come through his chambers and their lives solely placed into his hands. He now sat in his place at the front of the onlookers, with the crowd now following suit.

"This court is now in session. The case of His Majesty the King versus Beau Wainwright", the clerk said from his raised pedestal. He looked at the judge and received a nod of approval to continue.

"Mr Beau Wainwright, you are charged that on the 13th of November 1939 at 23 Wrenford Street, London, you did murder Mr John Foster, Mrs Eden Foster, Master Jim Foster & Miss Clare Foster. How do you plead, guilty or not guilty?"

The courtroom stayed silent. If any of those names or allegations shocked anyone in the room, it didn't show. In fact, this case had been regarded as one of the biggest upcoming trials in the last few decades. Reporters would line both the inside and the outside of the courthouse every day, attempting to get any glimpse or comment from the defendant as he was shrouded in cloth as he would move from the police van to the building.

"Not guilty." Beau Wainwright said, only just loud enough for the judge and jury to hear.

Beau looked like a man who had given up on life, not caring about the true outcome of his trial and if he was actually found guilty or not. By this point, his heart no longer raced at the inability to understand the situation he was in. He felt betrayed by his own body and its lack of energy for anything in this life. His eyelids drooped as he sat, barely able to lift his arms to even itch his nose.

The clerk turned from Beau and now faced the Jury, "How say you, gentlemen of the jury, are you sworn?"

The clerk was a young man, perhaps in his late twenties had a significant responsibility for such a young man. He was clearly sharp and charismatic in most instances. However, in this case, he fumbled over his words and the clear look of terror from doing so noticeably affected him. The jury was, in fact, composed of eleven men and one woman. In the thirties, it was quite rare for women to sit in the jury box alongside men in a court, but not completely unheard of. The woman sitting among her peers was a stark contrast in comparison. The men, all white, in black suits with fedoras blended in with the normalcy of these times. Whereas the woman wore a long, slim, red dress, which fell to her ankles, with a black feather boa covering her neck and shoulders.

"Uh, oh, my apologies", he stuttered, "gentlemen and lady of the jury." The clerk cleared his throat.

He went to the sidebar and picked up a Bible. Taking it to the first man, juror number one, with a sour scowl on his face, the clerk asked him to put his hand on the Bible and swear.

"I swear by Almighty God that I will faithfully try the defendant and give a true verdict according to the evidence", juror number one said, before the clerk moved on to every other juror.

After only two days of testimony, the trial was over. Although no motives were found, the evidence was clear and the prosecutor had it in the bag. Beau Wainwright was sentenced on the 14th of December 1939, at the age of thirty-three, to death.

Beau Wainwright, still without a single word beyond "not guilty", stood up in court, was shackled and led away, the only sound coming from the thick chains dangling from his ankles. He was on his way to his new home at Pentonville Prison.

&

Beau didn't have the same luxury this time as he was led to the police van without his veil of cloth. His face, photographed by every news reporter from around the countryside, guaranteed he wouldn't be forgotten for quite some time, dead or not.

He entered the police vehicle from the rear. A young police officer followed him in and sat staring at him from the other side of the van. Beau looked at the young policeman in the eye, perhaps a sign of jealousy passing over his thoughts as in such a small room. They both sat in silence, fidgeting with one thing or another as the van bumped along the cobblestone roads. The young policeman finally looked like he gained some courage when twenty-five minutes into their thirty-minute journey, he spoke.

"What do you think it'll be like?" the young officer said.

"I don't know."

The policeman nodded, acting like that was a perfectly valid answer to the question he had asked.

"What are you going to do?" He asked another question.

Beau stayed silent, his head remained positioned down and his eyes settled onto the floor, watching as a lone beetle crawled along the front of his polished courtroom shoes.

The view of Pentonville Prison littered the landscape as the tall, white wall grew larger as they drove closer to the surrounding outer limits of the prison grounds. The bus stopped at the first gate. A guard with a mirror on a stick circled the perimeter of the van, looking for anything illegal trying to be smuggled in. He waved at the driver to say, 'Okay, you're good to go,' and opened the gate.

The van arrived at the front of the prison, perfectly fitting into a white square, designated just for offloading the murderous criminal in the back of the van. The sound of a lock was heard outside the van before the doors swung open onto two more police officers waiting for him.

The smell of musty, stale water filled the nostrils of both the detainee and the young policeman as it wafted into the back of the van.

Beau climbed out into the damp air, looked over his new home before turning back towards the officer and looked at him with one last sorrow-filled look.

The policeman opened his mouth to say something. The cogs moved around in his mind as though he had all the time in the world. "Good luck, Boone".

Boone put a slight smile on his face, not a happy one, but enough to say 'Thanks'.

"And you, Dunlop."

Chapter Two

Boone shivered as he took his first steps into the main wing of the prison. The room he entered was impossibly long, with double-storied cells and a single metal staircase in the centre. The numbered cells ran the length of the room above peeling white-painted doors. The wing was eerily silent from a strictly enforced rule of no noise or talking. No one would dare put their life at risk just to crack a joke.

"Mr Wainwright, you have been assigned cell number four-zero-five in the condemned suite. You will stay and live in this cell henceforth until you are then taken to the gallows for execution. You will be given two meals daily. If you break the rules, such as talking, you will be forgotten about for supper that day."

The guard said all that without looking once at Boone. He said it in such a way that made it seem like this was an everyday occurrence. To him, simply Boone being there still alive was putting a damper on his day.

Boone stepped into a brick, box-shaped cell. It was no larger than he was long and not wide enough to stretch both arms out fully. The room was bare, apart from a bucket in the room's corner and a bed with no pillow. A Bible lay solo on the middle of the bed, his only reading selection for the remainder of his life. Without the laughs, cries or chatter of the room, the scraping of boots was the only thing that could be heard. The guard walked away down the hallway, leaving Boone alone with his thoughts.

Boone listened for the last sounds of the guard's boots moving away from his cell and out of the wing. He paused, almost like he were a statue, waiting for someone to come poke him to see if he were real. His eyes went from side to side, like he was looking out for someone else who may have hidden themselves in the corner of his claustrophobic cell. His hand went to his mouth and pulled out a thin metal rod the length of his hand. He immediately bent over and started to pick the lock of his ankle shackles, counting as he did it.

"One, two, three, four...." *CLICK*, "New record, not bad, Boethius".

Boone wasn't new to this; he'd been escaping situations for years. Of course, being in a prison in 1939 was going to be a new challenge for him. This wasn't the first prison that Boone had seen himself in, nor would it be the last, he figured. Over the years that he had been roaming the earth, he had found himself in some of the worst conditions imaginable. His last major sentence was in the 1300s in Bastille Saint-Antoine, Paris, which made Pentonville Prison look like a dream. Nevertheless, the torture of solitude may end up being the same. Still, the death because of disease would be exponentially slimmer, assuming he planned on lasting more than the two to three weeks before his execution.

Boone slipped his shackles off his feet and immediately started to look around the room with not only his eyes, but his hands and feet. He was feeling for every brick, every steel bar, anything that would help him out of this situation. His heart raced as he thought about when the next guard might be walking by to inspect the prisoners, billy club in hand. It was almost the middle of winter, but he started to sweat. He searched high and low for absolutely anything that might indicate a flaw, something that could give him a glimmer of hope in such a depressing place.

Boone had checked everything, going from top to bottom. He was going over his last little section of the roof with the metal rod he used to pick open his shackles. It went through. The metal rod, barely bigger than the thickness of a fingernail, drove straight through a soft section of the roof of Boone's cell. He laughed a quick 2 yelps, forgetting the rule of silence.

A door was heard opening and then quickly slamming as the sound of heavy boots stomping came from the dark corridor towards his cell. He quickly jumped off the bed, put his ankle shackles back onto his legs as quietly as he could and sat, pretending to read the Bible. The guard stopped only a few paces away, looking into each cell, wanting to find a reason to beat down the spirits of his onlookers. Without a word, he slammed his billy club into the steel bar of the cell just opposite Boone. He stared at its occupant for thirty long seconds before leaving the room once again, slamming the door.

Boone counted out another thirty seconds after he left and let out a sigh of relief with goose bumps appearing all over his body. He looked up and seeing the small hole in the roof, he smiled.

That evening was rough. The bed was hard, the lights were on constantly. The rats were the only sound that came out of the whole building, only being scared away by the constant patrol of guards rattling up the corridor. By this stage in life, Boone had become accustomed to the luxuries of modern-day living. Although he had spent many years of his life moving from one place to the next and didn't always have a bed to crawl into or a roof to hide under. Like anyone else, he also dreamt of a cozy bed and a thick blanket to crawl into at night.

He didn't sleep that night; in fact, he planned on sleeping as little as he could. You see, he figured that he had between two and three weeks before his execution came up and he was dragged to the gallows. This meant, at that time, he needed to study the guards, their movements and their alertness. He didn't always see the guards, so he had to label each one based on the sound of their distinct walking patterns. Studying the guards gave him the information he needed to know. Like when to make the hole bigger or stay completely silent on his bed. The age-old saying of 'A chain is only as strong as its weakest link' plays particularly strongly when it comes to warders of the prison.

Boone spent that night and several more doing just that. He had nowhere to write, so most of the retained information was squarely placed in his head.

He knew that Warder A was a heavy step. He walked with purpose, moving quickly from one cell, spending less than half a second looking in, before moving to the next. He got through the whole wing in less than five minutes. Warder B was a lighter step, almost cat-like if it weren't for a slight dragging of his boot as he moved it forward, lifting it into the air. He was slow in walking, but didn't spend any time pausing, looking into the cells, almost like he was just going on a casual stroll through the park. Warden C was the most unpredictable. He would often come into the wing with a swing in his step and move to the first cell, saying good morning or good night, chatting briefly and then moving on to his next favourite prisoner. Warder C was named Jimmy Black. He was a thin man of average build, probably with a young wife and two kids at home waiting for him to return every evening, dinner waiting for him on the table. He was also the happiest, perhaps to the disgust of the people he watched over.

"Beau", Jimmy said to him, leaning against his cell.

"Yeah, Gov?" Boone replied, sitting up from his bed.

"How you settling in?" He asked almost like it were just any other day.

Boone looked at him, not like a stranger, an acquaintance or even a friend. Boone looked inside, cutting off all his other senses around him and saw a pure white radiating from Jimmy's chest. Almost like someone had just blown out a candle and the last remnants of smoke were floating away into nothingness.

Boone snapped back, "Oh, you know."

Jimmy nodded his head, almost as if to say he understood the feeling of being on death's door, which, of course, he didn't.

How he interacted with the other prisoners, Boone knew that Jimmy was a good man. He gave them his time and treated them like they were actual humans, rather than just scum for the other warders to flick off the bottom of their boots. Jimmy might not have understood, knowing what it felt like to be part of the condemned, but he was empathetic and that's what made him the most human out of the whole prison.

It would have been so easy for Boone to allow the short-term friendship to fill in his last days alive; at least he wouldn't have been so lonely. However, what Boone needed most at this time was to be left alone.

Chapter Three

The next seven days were spent much the same for Boone. Wait for the warder's shift change, which he knew happened once Warder B had an extra spring in his step, knowing his last rounds were about to finish. Then Warden C, Jimmy, was about to start. This was generally around the same time as the sun began to set in the west.

Once the changeover had happened, Boone had approximately ten minutes. He needed to remove his shackles, get onto his bed and then dig away as much as he could at the roof. All of this before hearing the door of the wing open again for the next inspection. He would have to count as closely as he could to the ten-minute mark without getting distracted. This wasn't always easy and more than half the time, Boone would forget about the counting and have to cut the digging short, making his progress slower than he would have liked.

By the second week, he estimated he was about halfway between life and death, in sentence terms. He needed to pick up the pace considerably, but had no way of doing so. He thought about trying to create some kind of riot. Or maybe even acting mentally incapable. But, he put that off as being too risky when it came to having to move from his cell. The days dragged. Each minute in the cell felt like an hour going by, as all he could do was wait for night to come, when there would only be one warder. He spent as much of his time as he could sleeping. Even with this, his mind chose not to shut down and treated his dreams as an opportunity to remind him of his upcoming doom.

Days eight, nine and ten skipped by like the rest. The hole in his roof was getting larger and larger. To a point where he was able to almost fit his body through it at that stage. The good thing about being part of the condemned was that, most of the time, you were left alone. Because you didn't leave your cell at any point during your stay, there was no reason or need for the warders or anyone else to come in and search you or inspect your area. This meant that although there was an obvious large hole, it wasn't noticed.

Beyond the hole in the roof was the inner workings of the prison wing. Boone didn't have a plan for when he was through, nor did he know what was on the other side. He figured the biggest hurdle would have been the cell, with the second being getting over the main walls.

On the eleventh day, moments after the sun had set and Jimmy was now the warder for the night, Boone got started once again on his hole. Jimmy had just made his first round of inspection and headed out the door of the wing to sit down and put his feet up. Boone was out of his shackles and had just cleared enough space in the roof to fit his body through. He reached up and felt the support beams inside the roof. Grabbing onto those, he pulled himself up and out of his cell.

His heart raced. This new progress in his escape had given him such a sense of relief, all he wanted to do was lie down and shut his eyes, but he couldn't. He looked around the new space. Above the cells ran a bare-walled walkway going from one end of the wing to the other. There were little holes with glass panes slotted in, which ran every few steps along the whole outer wall of the walkway. It was tight, barely enough for Boone's shoulders to fit in if he were facing towards one end. He was not a tall man, but still had to bend down slightly as he stood. He put a smile on his face for the first time since arriving at Pentonville.

Just as Boone went to take a step towards one end of the walkway, he heard a commotion below him. The door to the wing swung open and slammed as it connected with the inner wall of the condemned living area. He immediately thought they'd caught him and were running to his cell at that very moment. He turned and jumped down the hole, not thinking about anything underneath it. He slammed against the edge of the bed, sending him off balance and smashing his head into the front wall of the cell, sending him unconscious.

An unknown amount of time later, his consciousness came into focus and he could hear talking. His eyes were still shut, afraid of what might be facing him on the other side of this.

Maybe the gallows, he thought. Perhaps they've brought up the date because they caught me. I can't die, not now, not after all this time for something I didn't do.

He opened his eyes and although it was blurry, he could see the familiar sight of his cell wall. Rubbing his eyes for a time, he cleared his vision and noticed that after scratching his head he had blood on his hands and it was trickling down his face, just passing his left ear. His body was twisted, like a freshly baked pretzel and hoped he hadn't broken anything other than his skin. He started to untangle himself, then pushed himself off the ground and onto the hard bed.

He sat for a moment, still trying to clear his head. He suddenly realised there was a mumbling of voices coming from just outside his cell in the corridor wing. He stood up and went to look at who it was.

He saw a group of four men standing around talking with serious looks on their faces. Definitely not your everyday sight to have in the prison. Boone's eyes were slightly blurry and his head hadn't fully recovered, but he could see at least who two of the men were. There was Jimmy, the night warder and Warder A, who Boone now knew was Frank Waltson. They were talking to a bigger man who looked like he demanded authority. He wore a large brown suit with an overcoat slung over his shoulders and his defining feature was his abnormally large eyebrows, which would have almost covered half his face if a cartoonist were to draw him.

Boone guessed him to be the Chief Warder or even the Governor of the prison, definitely someone not to be messed with.

The fourth man was interesting. He stood off to the side, a half-stride away from the other warders. His arms wrapped around himself, almost like he were giving himself a hug trying to comfort his own mind. He looked between the three who were talking, every now and then trying to interject and add something to the conversation. Each time he tried, someone would talk over him.

Boone rubbed his eyes a little as more focus became clearer and his brain became less and less foggy. He now noticed that the fourth man in fact wasn't a warder, but he was a prisoner, like Boone. He was dressed the same, in some dirty brown loose-fitting slacks and top, with a pair of reading glasses perched gently on the edge of his nose.

The four men left the wing one after the other, with the mystery prisoner trailing closely behind. Boone shook his head, not really understanding what that was about, but glad it actually had nothing to do with him. He sat back on his bed, head now stinging from an open cut and pounding from the knock it caused. Boone lay down and fell asleep.

Chapter Four

"Hello!" A yell echoed from outside the cell.

Boone woke up with a fright, wondering what on earth was now going on, slightly angry from the sudden wake-up.

"Hello! Anyone!" The man yelled even louder, with a slight hint of desperation in those two words.

Boone slowly rolled over and his body ached. He had just spent the last ten days, arms stretched above him, digging out a hardened concrete roof, jumping up and down every nine minutes to avoid the guards. The pain from doing that had subsided by the fifth day. But this pain, this fresh new pain, was worse. His mind scoured through his entire body to check he hadn't broken a bone, which he hadn't. The damage he suffered was simply soft tissue. Both his legs, his left arm, along with the stinging cut on the top left of his skull, made him wince internally as he touched them.

Pain was nothing new to Boone. A lifetime of falls, escapes, attacks by people or wild animals had hardened him overtime. This was just one of those things that the life of a Soul Keeper entailed. His early years were filled with travel as he crossed from one corner of the world to the next. A pain, which would forever be fresh in his mind was that of his first solo travel from Egypt to England. All completely on foot and with a significant chunk of his life missing.

At this time, several different empires spanning across different continents ruled this part of the world. He lived in Egypt for a short time, roughly twenty years. Falling under the rule of Fatimid Caliphate of the Islamic Shia empire. He went by Bashir Al-Misri, a travelling merchant who sold papyrus scrolls of news from one region to the next. He was known to all in the area as 'Bashir the Golden' for his news of fluctuating prices for precious metals, cotton or spices. Of course, he acted as a middleman for a lot of trades over the twenty years, accumulating major wealth and reputation. This reputation came with safety when travelling through the rural regions, giving donations to any villages he crossed. This was the start of what he hoped was a two-year journey across what is now known as Europe.

Once Boone had left the Fatimid Caliphate, he walked north through the Anatolia region, now known as Turkey. This was ruled by the Macedonian dynasty, which was part of the Eastern Roman Empire. It started out tough with him realising that during most of his travel through this region, he would be stopped over and over again through border zones. Constant pressure from people suggesting he was a spy became the norm very quickly. The first few stops through border zones would sometimes take hours, but others took days. Mostly being kept in overheated and overcrowded cells, he learnt from others what to say or not to say as the times passed. He would always eventually be released. By the sixth stop, he knew he needed a back-story. This is where he named himself Basileios of Antioch, a Roman scholar. He told them he was travelling through to monasteries to bring them the word of the world and of God.

The Romans were loyal to their empire. They couldn't be bribed with gold or sold on lies. They needed to believe everything you were telling them in order to get through to the next region. Boone told them stories; he was good at that at his age. He told them things about God and people, about the lands in the faraway parts of the world and the harsh travels. He carried on with this from stop to stop, resting for a day or two between each. Eventually, word got ahead of him that a strange man was telling the word of travels, that he was all knowledgeable and powerful.

By the time Boone had travelled through the whole of Anatolia and reached Constantinople, the word of Basileios had spread. People would often see him and point, mentioning him as somewhat of a god. According to the people there, they had heard word of him taking down packs of wolves or a giant brown bear all by himself. Nobody dared to question the validity of that and Boone didn't argue.

Boone carried on, passing through the Balkans much the same as he did Anatolia. There was perhaps a bit more risk of Bandits who he could give a donation of gold to, avoiding any further problems. The story of Basileios, the Scholar, mostly faded once he was halfway through. Most of the travel got colder and harsher as he went and found himself more in solitude. He found extensive forests of dense vegetation or fallen logs. Struggling to get through even a small portion of it, he purchased an iron sword from one of the bandit camps. This helped him get through most of it.

Once he reached the Alps, the danger wasn't so much from the people or the animals. It was the cold and snowy weather that slowed him down. He followed the pilgrim trails for most of it, stopping over in monasteries at mountain outposts or river valleys. The monks at the outpost would provide hospitality to him, give him food and prayers. He sometimes spent months at these monasteries, helping them farm or cook. Even helping them build simple stone buildings or teaching them new techniques from the outside world.

Once the warmer months came around, Boone moved on from the monks and headed towards northern France. The journey through France was meant to be the safest he had been during his whole journey. The country at the time was ruled by Robert the Pious. In smaller regions, dukes, counts and barons ran their own territories all over like their own mini kingdoms.

Boone's travels across the land could be tedious in a way. It wasn't uncommon for him to backtrack for safety reasons or out of concern. When entering what looked like a new region to him, he would quite often hide away or bury the clothes and wealth he travelled with. He'd trek forward a few hours and see the region was safe, walk back, pick up his gear and move on his way.

Before getting up to the most northern part of France, he scouted along the west coast. An attempt to find his way onto a boat and up to England. He found himself at a few ports, talking with local captains who mostly outright refused. Boone, being an outsider, had major disadvantages and as soon as he spoke, they didn't trust him.

Without a ride across the channel, Boone went back to travelling north. He entered into a region that he now knew as Anjou, ruled by a legendarily cruel bastard named Fulk the Black. He entered a particular region ruled by Fulk, where he was said to have a monastery where he was hoping to rest for a few weeks. As he got within earshot of the monastery, he heard the clanging of swords, the raging of fire and the screaming of women and children. The monastery and the surrounding village were being attacked and pillaged by Fulk's men. As soon as they saw Boone, they attacked him.

Boone was captured. It wasn't that he was carrying any obvious wealth with him; it wasn't that he was even carrying a weapon or trying to save anyone. It was simply because he looked different from anyone else around him. Fulk's men wanted to use him as a political prisoner, attempting to gain ransom or even leverage on those who might come looking for him. Without too much as three words between them, he was thrown into the underground dungeon of one of the castles that Fulk ruled over. Boone was left to die. The dungeon was grim, with no light or bedding. Food was slim at only a fraction of bread a day along with a bowl of water. Rats, lice and disease ran rampant amongst him and the other prisoners.

People died constantly from either open wounds or disease. Boone would often help them, ensuring their end wasn't painful or scary and so they knew they were moving on to something else. Fulk and his men waited for someone to have word of a man looking like Boone around the region. They waited days, then weeks and then eventually months. They were sure someone from somewhere would come looking. It never happened. He was held captive for ten years. The only reason that Boone was ever set free was because Fulk was eventually excommunicated and all the prisoners were set free, or at least those who survived.

The escape from France was important now. He needed to exit the region and traverse across the water to England. He made his way all the way back just south of Anjou, picked up his buried wealth and returned to the ports up north as fast as he could. Over the ten years of his capture, he had become fluent in Old French as well as Latin, almost to the extent that he could speak and act French. With this, he was able to secure transport across the water the same day he reached Normandy.

Boone arrived in England in short time and immediately purchased monk robes. He made the last two weeks of his journey all the way to London under the guise of a poor monk, travelling in the church lands, which was relatively safe.

This journey from Egypt to London took him thirteen years, but it felt like a lifetime. He swore never to do that again and didn't. At least not for the next few hundred years.

It might feel like Boone's travels stopped there and up until this moment, never made it out of London, but he did. For a long time, he treated London as his home. He loved the life-style and it was as safe as you would get in this area of the world. But now, with him sitting in the cell at Pentonville, he could no longer call it home. He had to escape. He had to leave the country.

"Help me!" The man's voice rang out one last time.

Chapter Five

The yelling of the man's voice, over and over again, drilled right through and into Boone's head. He rubbed his temples, begging for either the pain or the yelling to fade away.

"Stop it!" he yelled through gritted teeth as he stood to look through the cell bars into the wing.

Immediately, as though a warder had just been waiting for it to happen, the wing door once again swung open. It slammed against the inside of the corridor, leaving another mark for history to count.

"What's the problem, Boone?" Jimmy yelled. "You know the rules; no talking! I would hate to have to drag you out of that cell. Don't make me do that, son."

Boone's hands wrapped around the cold steel bars, looking at Jimmy as he spoke to him from only a step away from his cell. He heard the words that came out of his mouth, but took little notice of them. As Jimmy had talked, something else had caught Boone's attention. He simply nodded to Jimmy.

"Sorry, Gov, won't happen again", he said.

Jimmy walked away and Boone's head snapped back to the man who was now standing in the middle of the wing. This was the same man who was with the three other warders. However, this time, with his head cleared, Boone could see he wasn't quite of this realm. He was a soul.

The man yelled again, "Hello!"

"Pssp", Boone called over to the man before they locked eyes on each other.

The man ran over to Boone, thankful that someone had actually paid any attention at all to him. He looked confused and scared, like a lost child at the fair.

The man wore his prison gear with the number 48151 on it. A thin rimmed spectacles sat on the end of his nose, just above a perfect line of teeth, showing he didn't exactly scream 'prison inmate'.

"Oh, thank god. I have been trying to get the attention of absolutely anyone around here", he said with a formal dialect, a mix of Old English and Latin.

"I don't know what is happening. One moment I was in my cell, the next moment I felt like I was moving through the air until I found myself standing next to the young warder. He completely ignored me. But whenever I try to run, it's like something is pulling me back."

"You're dead", Boone said, very clearly and matter-of-fact. "You have died in your cell; you are bound to warder Jimmy until you are in your final resting place."

"Preposterous", the man said. "I am feeling completely fine. In fact, I feel better than I have in many, many years."

Boone nodded his head, realising now he should have slowly broken the news to him rather than just coming out and saying it.

"Okay, look, give me some time and I'll figure out what has happened. In the meantime, you should be able to stick around here until the sun starts to come up. I'll talk to you just before that."

"By the way, what do I call you?" Boone asked.

"Edmund", he replied sheepishly, before quietly walking off and trying to talk to the other prisoners on the wing.

Boone sighed, knowing that getting any information about this would drain him of energy. However, the payoff of someone who could potentially walk through walls would work well as a sidekick in his attempt to escape.

He went back to his bed and sat down, bringing up his legs and crossing them under him. Taking a few deep rhythmic breaths, he shut his eyes and closed off the remainder of his senses around him.

Time on this earth had allowed Boone to somewhat easily train his body into a meditative state, separating his mind from his body. With his eyes closed, he heard the world around him. The scattering of rats and falling cockroaches, the cold, damp air circulating through the cell, the hard wooden bed knocking against his ankles and the smell of death and sewage which hung in the air.

His mind went blank; everything was gone and all he could see was a white glow from the surrounding walls. The room turned from a soft humming vibration into a large rumble. A violent shaking started as cracks in the white glowing walls opened as though everything around him smashed into a million little pieces. He opened his eyes.

Boone stood looking across the street from Berkeley Court, a large eight-story brick flat. He was back in London. He looked at the moon, estimating he had roughly three hours to get back to the prison, back to his body.

He walked across the street and into the building lobby, eyeing the doorman as he walked straight past him. Inside the building, he walked towards the stairs and made his way up to the third floor and straight to flat 23, which was tucked around the corner at the end of the hallway. Boone stood for a moment and waited.

The door opened wide from the inside, showing a sad-faced, quiet man.

"Hello, mate", said Dunlop.

"Hello, James", Boone replied.

"You better come in. I thought I could feel you coming. Maggie thought I was going mad getting out of bed at four in the morning to open the front door."

"Thank you. How is Maggie? Tell her I appreciate her support at the trial. That can't have been easy for her."

Boone and Dunlop sat down in the family room of the flat, a fireplace now lit with Dunlop rubbing his hands in front of it, trying to keep warm.

"Where are you now?" Dunlop asked.

"Sitting in my cell at Pentonville still. That's kind of why I needed to talk with you. I have a soul tethered to one of the warders down there, Jimmy Black. I need to know how he died and when the funeral is. I'm through the ceiling and into some kind of walkway above the prison. If you can find out any information about that, that would be helpful."

Just then, Dunlop's wife, Maggie, walked into the room rubbing the sleep from her eyes. She noticed the fire was on.

"Is he here?" She asked, unable to see Boone sitting on one of the single couches right in front of her.

"Hello Darling. Yes, Boone is here", he said, pointing to the couch. "We're just having a chat about the prison. You go back to bed", he continued. He kissed her lips, which told her he'd be back in bed soon.

Boone and Dunlop spent the next few hours talking about mostly the Prison, layouts, the investigation and the eventual funeral for Edmund, Jimmy's tethered soul. At the end of their time, Boone looked out the window and knew he needed to get back. They stood up and shook hands, but no physical connection was felt between either of them. In the blink of an eye, Boone was gone.

In no less than one second, his senses came back again and he was back in the prison at Pentonville. The usual damp smell immediately came back to him, almost like an unwelcoming home gift.

"Bloody hell, Edmund!" Boone said, as his eyes opened to Edmund's face staring directly into his eyes. They both got a fright as neither was expecting the other to be there.

"Bloody hell, yourself! I thought you had just died while sitting there!" Edmund responded.

Boone stood up. "Okay, I'm waiting for someone to give me some information about your death. Until then, I need you to search around, tell me what you see and hear. Go with Jimmy and see what their office is like. I need as much information as you can give."

Edmund nodded his head and walked towards and through the iron bars of Boone's cell. The fact of his death looked like it had finally settled into his mind and he accepted it.

Death isn't the same for everyone. The pain and the trauma of it can be taken away by touch and the soul being tethered to someone can help them. Sometimes the tether is aware; other times he is not. The universe gives only what is needed in the time you need it. The idea of Edmund roaming around still, while Jimmy doesn't show any signs of acknowledgement of that, gives the idea that the universe gave Edmund to Boone for help.

Ideas, regrets, jealousy and any of the seven deadly sins are all felt by certain souls. The person who they were before the death can often dictate that by bringing their good or bad energy through to this realm. If a good person dies, they often have regret or sorrow for those they have left behind. If a bad person dies, they bring through vengeance and wrath for those left behind. If an evil person dies, they can haunt and cause chaos to the world around them, even to the point of refusing to move on after their final resting place.

The sun came up that morning before Boone got to see Edmund again. Of course, being tethered to Jimmy meant that he would be travelling home with him and spending a good portion of the day waiting for Jimmy to wake up.

By the time the sun started to set, Boone could hear Edmund yelling through the door of the wing to let him know that he was there, but he wasn't yet able to get to him. Thirty minutes later, they were side by side.

"Now that is strange. It's like I was just a spy walking through his house, watching his every move. His wife and kids didn't even see me!"

"Of course, now tell me what you learnt." Boone was straight to the point and didn't want to waste time he didn't have.

"Okay, here we go. The walkway above you runs fifty paces north before turning towards the south and down a set of stairs completely outside, which means it'll be easy for you to get down. The problem is you run straight into the main guardhouse, so I'd say that's not great. The walkway also runs around seventy paces to the north, looping around to the other side of the wing. But before you get to the other side, there is a hatch which leads into the guard's room for the condemned wing."

Just as Edmund finished that last sentence, the room startled to ripple, but only for a few seconds before Dunlop came into view, standing in Boone's cell next to them.

"Dunlop", Boone said.

Edmund's jaw dropped. He knew he was dead, but had never experienced anything like this in his time alive. He couldn't believe what he was seeing, so much so that he didn't say a single word to either Dunlop or Boone.

"I don't have long as I haven't been taking reserves from Keeps lately", Dunlop said.

He went into detail with Boone and Edmund listening in. The funeral of Edmund had not been set. Since Edmund was a prisoner, no one had claimed his body yet. This meant that if the Prison was to bury him, that could be in less than a day, even a few hours away. With this short timeframe, any information that Dunlop had about the investigation wasn't useful to him. Boone had to escape today.

"Okay, Edmund, we're going to do this quick, so you need to be my look-out and give me every detail along the way. I will go into the roof walkway, down the hatch into the guard's room and leave via that way. You need to find out for me what is beyond the guard's room. That is what I need you to do."

With that, Boone set a time limit of thirty minutes before the escape.

"One last thing", Edmund said. He paused, almost like he didn't want to ask the question. "Who are you?"

"My name is Boethius. I am a Soul Keeper."

Chapter Six

Jimmy Black entered the wing of the condemned, just like every other day he had worked there. He walked along the cells, swinging his billy club as he whistled, not realising that a happy whistle was not for the condemned.

Not once in the thirty years since it had been built had anyone ever escaped. Today was different. Today, Jimmy walked his last walk inside this prison. After this, he would be labelled as incompetent and promptly fired. Of course, who could have known that a very old man and his ghost accomplice would do such a thing on this very day, at this very moment?

Boone took three breaths as he heard the wing door close after Jimmy's ten-minute inspection of the cell block. The second after the door was closed, Boone reached down and for hopefully the last time, unlocked his ankle shackles. He slid them off, climbed onto his bed and was in the roof in less than twenty seconds.

The plan was simple; Boone would work his way out and Edmund would yell the whole time, giving him updates along the way, letting him know where Jimmy was.

"He's sitting down!" Edmund yelled. Boone was only just able to hear him through the thick concrete walls.

Boone was on the walkway. He looked south, noting the way to the guardhouse. He carried on north towards the break room for the condemned wing warders. The walkway was made of hardened steel and was surrounded on each side by more of the same concrete brick that covered the whole prison over. There were opening gaps in the wall, which showed the outside as he walked further north.

Reaching the seventy paces, he turned left and came upon a hatch, just as Edmund had described it. It was large and was obviously there as an access point between safety areas in case of lockdowns. There were six latches on it that looked like they needed a screwdriver to get through.

"You should see a piece of broken-off steel. It looks like it came from a stairwell or something. You should be able to use that to hook onto the latches; they just need a ninety-degree turn upwards!" Edmund yelled up at Boone.

Boone looked around, trying to see what he was talking about, finding it only a few seconds later. He used the tool as quietly as he could, undoing the first of the six latches. Boone heard movement from below as the first latch made a creaking sound from years of disuse.

"Gov heard that! He's blaming it on rats! I don't think you'll get away with that again!" Edmund yelled.

It was the middle of winter and temperatures were dropping to below zero, yet Boone was sweating profusely. The idea of this failing was almost certainly a guaranteed death upon being captured. It didn't matter how long he had been around or what skills he had learnt over time. If he was caught, there would be nothing he could do about it. Even to a Soul Keeper, death is death.

Nevertheless, he carried on with opening the latches; the second one popped open easier than the last, but just as loudly. He then went to the third one and popped it open. He heard the noise of a chair scraping on the ground from below. It was obvious by now that Jimmy was out of his chair and perhaps inspecting the roof, listening out closer for the next creak or pop.

"He's standing up, Boone", Edmund said in a whisper, almost as if he yelled, he would be heard and caught himself.

Suddenly, there was the sound of the wing door swinging open and boots were heard running towards the condemned cells.

"He's in the wing! You need to get down or back to your cell!"

Boone flicked the last three latches on the hatch and pulled it up, exposing the inside of the warder break area. He put his head through, noticing that the door to the wing was wide open. Bringing his head back up, he spun around and lowered himself feet first before lowering his body onto a perfectly placed table just below the hatch.

He ran for the door to the wing, entering the corridor so he could reach the handle of the door. He locked eyes with Jimmy and they both stopped completely still. Jimmy slowly reached down towards his hip, where he kept his gun. Almost as though if he moved slowly enough, Boone wouldn't see him.

"I'm sorry, Jimmy", Boone said. "This has to happen."

Boone pulled the door to the cell and ducked down, just as Jimmy pulled out his revolver from the holster and fired it toward Boone, only barely missing. With the door shut, he used the metal rod to jam the handle and frame, making it almost impossible for the warder to get back through. Boone turned around and saw Edmund standing directly behind him, his hand on his heart and shock on his face.

"He shot me", he said with an ache in his voice. "He shot me, Boone."

"You're dead, Edmund, you can't be shot, you can't die any more than you currently are."

Edmund uncovered his heart and looked towards his chest to see a completely fine, intact and holeless chest.

"Come on, we need to get going", Boone said, before realising a critical mistake in his plan.

"Shit! You can't come with me; you're tethered to Jimmy." He thought for a second. "Tell me everything you know about what is outside this door." Boone pointed towards the door that led towards the main admin building of the prison.

Although Jimmy was locked in the wing with the other prisoners, they had time. In his haste to work out what or who was above in the crawl space, Jimmy ran into the corridor without picking up his radio. Boone gave a little "Thanks" under his breath before tucking it into the lining of his slacks.

"Okay, so just outside this door is another corridor, which goes both left and right. They both end up in the same location, but if you go right, you'll run into a couple of warders who look like they're chatting about the phoney war. Apparently, more soldiers are going over for no reason. What you really need to do is wait for one of them to come past and knock him out to steal his uniform!" Edmund suggested.

"No, that's not going to happen. I'll find a uniform, but I'm not hurting anyone for it."

"Suit yourself. Anyway, once you go left, you'll pass by a couple of extra rooms and then reach the end of that corridor, where you'll see the door for the main admin building. This is a room filled with desks and typewriters but only a couple of men are in there, just talking. Unfortunately, that's as far as I can get before I feel the pull back to the gov in the wing."

Boone took that all on and immediately started to rummage through the cupboards and drawers. He was looking for anything that might help him but hoping for at least an employee uniform of some kind. Not worrying about the mess, he didn't care too much about leaving things out, but he needed to be quiet. He wasn't sure how common it was for others to enter the room if they had nothing to do with this wing.

"Okay, I have no choice", he said to Edmund. "I'm going to make a break for the next room. Thank you for your help, Edmund. All the best with what is next with you."

Over his life, Boone had seen hundreds of thousands of souls. Most of who he would talk to or have some kind of quiet connection with. He tried to be as empathetic as he could for everyone, but he had to read the people first. There were mothers who had died, who knew they were never going to see their children again; they needed the human connection the most. Then there were people who would die alone, at home in their rocking chairs, barely having seen a human over the last month. Some were happy to move on to their next life; others didn't want to leave what they had.

Edmund was slightly different. He had peeked under the curtain of what this world entails, energy transfers and movement of people's essence. He knew that whatever was waiting for him next was okay. He was ready to move on. Of course, he didn't say this, but Boone felt it.

Boone reached for the door to the outer corridor and opened it just enough to see through a small gap in it. He could see that the two warders who Edmund had talked about must have been still around the corner. He opened up the door slightly more before slipping out into the larger area. He closed the door behind him, which made a slight creaking noise as it snibbed into place. Boone stood still, almost like he was afraid of what he might turn around to see. Nothing forcefully grabbed him on the shoulder, so he started slowly walking to the left.

He walked, inching his way as got closer towards the corner. He peeked around and saw the coast was clear, so carried on. Getting to the first door, he took the risk of opening it. He reached for the door handle and pushed it down and in, almost like he was opening the door to someone's bedroom, afraid of waking them. With only just enough room, he put his head through the door gap and froze.

"Alright, keeping busy?" Boone said, now face on with two warders who must have been on patrol for another wing in the prison. Lucky for Boone, they hadn't seen his prison uniform.

The two in the room looked at each other, almost to say, "Who's this then?". "Steady night, mate. You alright?" one of the men asked.

"Yeah, mate", Boone replied before shutting the door again. The awkward conversation between the three couldn't have been any worse if they had tried.

He hoped that nothing he did or said made them second-guess who he was or what he was doing there. He picked up his pace a little as he moved onto the second room, hoping that there wasn't going to be another instance of that happening again.

Boone ran into the best luck he could have asked for. He opened the door, popped his head in and saw that he was in the warders' changing room. He quickly opened the door wider and closed it behind him. Leaning on the inside of the door, he took a deep breath and let it out slowly. His heart was racing, knowing that at any moment, the two from next door could come in.

He started searching for what he needed, which didn't take long. Finding a spare pair of slacks and a shirt worn by the warders in the prison, he quickly put them on and found that they fit perfectly. Without a second to waste, he clipped Jimmy's radio back onto his waist and left the room.

He carried on down the corridor until he reached the doorway which Edmund had told him about, the one with all the desks. Boone was thankful that it was nighttime and none of the women secretaries would have been sitting at their desks. He could feel his heart racing as he then opened the door with as much confidence as he could muster up.

In the room were two more men dressed in slightly different uniforms from the warders who were watching over the prisoners. Boone could only guess, but he thought these men might have been part of the watch team or those who kept watch of the fence lines or entry points.

"Alright, lads", Boone said as he carried on walking towards them, aiming for the doorway just past both of them.

They both just stared at Boone for what felt like minutes. "Who are you then?" said one of the men. Boone felt like he had just been caught and this was the end.

"Jimmy is training me for the condemned wing. He's just hit the lav and he's run out of paper, just going to grab some because the stock room is out."

Boone had been around long enough to train himself in certain techniques, including confusing the enemy or attempting to take over the conversation or get as much information out of them as he could. He used these techniques as a last resort, as they didn't always work.

Before the men had even one second to speak up, Boone continued. He reached out to shake both of the men's hands. "Frank Baker", he said confidently. "You are?" Boone pointed to one of the men. A finger is like a magic wand; you can get almost any information you want just by asking a question, pointing, and staying silent. Unless they're trained not to give out information, they would immediately be on the front foot trying to answer.

"Oh, uh, Harry Williams", the first one said. Without saying a word, Boone moved his finger towards the second man.

"John Richardson".

"Fantastic. Great to meet you both! How long had you been working here?" Boone's finger went up again at Harry.

"Uh, six months for both of us."

"Six months, huh? You lads are young; you're not joining the army and heading over to the war?"

Boone didn't want to give them even one second of time to ask their own questions back at him. Before even letting them answer that question, he said.

"Sorry, lads. Gotta run, will chat soon." He patted John on the back as he walked directly past them and through the door into the next room. Once again, Boone's heart raced as he knew that all it would take was one doubt from either of the men and they would follow him.

He stood in another corridor, this one with a completely locked fence right in front of him and a night watchman standing over to the side in a little booth. The guard walked out, looking at Boone with the same quizzical look as everyone else had given him so far.

"Afternoon, just getting a message out for Warder Williams", Boone said, hoping that would make at least some sense to the watchman.

He eyed Boone up and down, obviously wondering how this person who he hadn't ever seen before was now exiting the prison he watched over.

"Wait there", he said in a harsh tone, before going back to his books, barely taking his eyes off Boone.

He picked up the logbook in front of him and ran his finger along each line as he went, taking roll call in his mind as he went line by line. Boone knew this was the end. He looked around the room for any other ideas or escape plans, but nothing was there. He decided he wasn't going to hurt this man for just doing his job.

"I can't find you here", the watchman said, eyeing Boone, inviting an explanation. None came. "I'm going to have to call the governor and see what is happening right now."

The watchman walked to the red phone that hung on a wall only a few paces away from where the watchman would have normally sat. He picked it up and began to rotate the dial as the door opened behind Boone.

"Frank! You're still here", Harry Williams said, coming from the previous room.

The watchman stopped his dialling and looked at Williams. "You know this warder, Harry?"

"Yeah, he's doing some work with Jimmy in the condemned wing", Williams said, almost as a matter of fact.

"He's not in the book", the watchman said.

Everyone stayed silent, almost like no one had an answer to any of the questions that hung in the air.

"When did you enter?" the watchman asked.

Boone knew what the watchman was trying to understand. He was starting to think that someone had messed up and he was hoping it wasn't himself. Boone needed to get the burden off the current watchman and put it onto whoever was before him.

Luckily, due to the timing of the warders in the condemned wing, he had a fairly good idea about the staff change.

Boone loosened up at this stage, knowing he now had a better chance of convincing the watchman.

"Oh mate, it was before sundown a few hours ago. I've left my watch at home, so I don't actually know what time it is now."

The watchman had a sigh of relief, almost to say he was glad it wasn't him that messed up.

"Alright", he said as he fished a set of keys from his waist and walked over to the gate. "Next time, you sign in correctly. You almost made me wake up the Gov for this."

Boone nodded an understanding to the watchman and walked out the now-opened gate. Once he was through and out the front door, he realised that there were no more locked doors or gates between him and the free world. He walked into an open area between the main admin building and the outer wall. He looked left and right and could see what looked like an endless white fence, adorned with circular barbed wire.

The front main gate was completely open with only one man watching over it. "Evening", Boone said as he walked through the gate and took his first step outside the main perimeter of the prison.

Boone took one last sigh of relief, just as a sudden and loud alarm rang from behind him.

"Shit!" was all Boone said as he looked behind him towards the inside of the admin building. He could see the watchman pointing towards him and fumbling for his keys.

Chapter Seven

Boone paused. His heartbeat from his chest was the fastest it had been this whole time. Both Boone and the watchman looked at each other, perhaps eyeing one another with a sense of suspicion.

"Huh, what do you think that is? Should we go in?" Boone asked.

The relief washed over the watchman, almost to show that a prisoner wouldn't have stayed around. The watchman stood from his seat and walked towards the main admin doors. He looked inside and saw that the watchman from inside was shouting and pointing behind him and yelling at him to "capture him!". The outside watchman turned around, his hand west to his waist, ready to aim. He lifted his gun and pointed it at nothing. Boone was gone.

At the very moment of the outdoor watchman turning and walking towards the admin building, Boone sprinted. He started running left, down what was signposted as Caledonian Road. He looked at the two-story buildings as he ran, looking for any kind of gap in the buildings he could run down. He didn't want to risk getting trapped in one of the buildings, so continued running until he met a crossroads. Tuning right down Frederica Street, he started to get further away from the prison. Running between flats, he eventually made it to some railway tracks. He could still hear the alarm of the prison and now the bells of police vehicles wailing in the distance on their way to the prison from all directions.

The tracks he found ran both north and south. It was night and because of the war, the train services were cut back because of blackout regulations and bombing risks. He looked up and down the tracks, wondering if there would be any underground sections in which he might be able to hide. He breathed rapidly and his mind was racing. He knew he was only minutes, if not seconds ahead of the search party behind him and he needed to make a choice.

Boone ran south down the tracks at a slower rate this time. He didn't have enough energy to keep up the pace he had been keeping. After two weeks of nothing but bread and water, there was nothing that was helping his body to regenerate the energy he had lost.

He could hear the officers and warders behind him yelling now, blowing their whistles as they came running in the same direction as him.

"Come on, Boethius, you can't be captured now", he said, trying to hype himself up.

He kept going at barely a running pace now, but was looking around for any place he could hide. In the distance, he saw a fire, small but contained, a familiar sight to be seen. He picked up his pace and jogged towards it.

"Evening", he said in a gruff voice to a homeless man who was hovering around the fire drum, warming his hands.

The man looked at him with a sour and weathered look on his face from many nights living on the streets.

Boone had spent a lot of his life living in the rough, sometimes because of his own choices and sometimes because of the universe's choice. In any case, he knew what it was like for these people; he knew their secret languages and the symbols they left behind to know it was safe. In fact, he had spent more time on the streets than this man could have in three lifetimes.

"Govs rough?" Boone asked the man, trying to get a read on him.

"It's safe. Kip where you like."

Boone nodded to the man, walking further into the camp where he saw more and more people lying on the ground or in self-made shelters. He picked up a woollen beanie, which seemed to be drying near another burning fire. He kept walking and picked up the jacket, which lay near a man clearly asleep. "I owe you one", Boone said quietly.

He slipped both the woollen beanie and jacket on and made his way deeper into the camp. Taking off his shoes, he gave them to another man who was sitting, staring at the ground. The man put a smile on his face, knowing he had just gotten some new shoes. Boone climbed behind the man and lay down in his shelter.

There was a certain protection that the homeless had with each other. The police were not to be consulted with, no matter what. Boone knew that if the police were to come around to the camp, there would be a high chance that not one of the homeless people would say anything, let alone the man who he had just given his shoes.

He could still hear the police bells still in the distance, knowing that they wouldn't be getting any closer as the roads don't come all the way to the tracks. He saw dozens of torches shining along the tracks coming towards the encampment of the homeless. Each torch acted like a little beacon, showing where they were looking and where they didn't care about. They passed by a manhole in the ground that Boone had considered. They looked at it with two torches and determined nothing was down there before moving on.

Boone closed his eyes. For one, he felt like he needed to pretend to be asleep; second to that, he had barely slept in days and was still recovering from the fall in his cell.

He could hear the warders and police asking questions as to whether someone had come into their camp. Most of the homeless had completely ignored them and didn't answer any questions. Some would talk and say no, or they didn't see anyone. The problem was that they were going to every single person in the camp, no matter what.

There were twelve police officers making their way down, person after person asking questions along the way. Boone opened his eyes slightly to see an older warder coming towards him; it was Warder A. He knew this was it and thought whether or not he should get up and run. He knew that he didn't have the strength in him to do so, but now they also had guns, something that they could just easily pull out and shoot Boone if he made even a slight movement.

As Warder A was coming towards Boone, another officer yelled at him. "I've got that one", he said.

Boone kept his eyes shut and heard the crunching of boots walk right up to him and stand right in front of him and crouch down.

"You alright?" the man asked.

He opened one eye and looked. It was Dunlop.

Boone's heart started to settle and the speed slightly dropped as he looked around and saw no one else coming up to him.

"I didn't feel you. I have no energy and can't close off my senses", Boone said.

"I figured. Stay low. I'll come get you in a few days once this is all blown over. We need to get you out of the city."

Boone agreed and he closed his eyes again and waited.

Hours passed and the sun started to rise, showing the entire camp and the countless people living without a roof over their heads. He could still see police positioned every few hundred metres going down the train tracks, just waiting for the escaped prisoner to pop his head up out of a hole in the ground, or at least they hoped.

Closing his eyes again, he put his head down once more so his head lay on the unwashed blanket below him. With the exhaustion still apparent from the previous day and the last two weeks on a hard wooden bed, it felt like he was sleeping on a cloud.

A low humming vibration sounded throughout the atmosphere. Boone instantly opened his eyes and sat up, slightly hunched over from the blankets that hung above his head protecting him from the cold.

Boone knew exactly what the hum was. It was the sense of death that hung in the air when someone was getting close to the end of their life. He had felt this a million times before, with it sometimes being his Keep, other times not. This time, strangely enough, it was not his.

From the low hum of the vibration and the clean resonance of it, he knew that whoever it was, had upwards of an hour to live and the death was going to be mostly easy for the person. He looked around the camp, moving his senses from one person to the next, trying to see the ripples around the unlucky person.

Homeless, tramps, vagrants, wayfarers, drifters, the list goes on. In 1939, life wasn't easy for these people and it wasn't uncommon for death to creep up on them due to starvation, disease, infection and murder. It was normal for at least one or two people to die per week in these camps, all across the country.

Boone stood up from the shelter and looked at the man whose home it used to be, who was still hovering around a small fire in front of him.

"Thanks for that", Boone muttered to the man.

The man nodded. "Fair trade, I'd say. Gov on your tail?"

"Whatever it is, I don't want to be caught up in it", Boone said. Trying to distance himself from the conversation.

The man pulled out a wooden box and sat it close to the fire, pointing Boone towards it. He gladly accepted the seat and warmed his hands in the fire, rubbing them over his face once they warmed up.

An hour later, a bunch of the homeless stood up and looked to see a girl coming from down the tracks. She had a cart with her that she pushed through the mud, struggling to get the wheels to move. One of the guys from the camp ran over to her and helped pull the cart by lifting it from one end. As the girl got closer, Boone could see her clearly. She was young, perhaps in her mid-twenties. She was only small at around five and a half feet and with a thin waist. She had red, orangey hair that hung down, barely touching her shoulders. She wore a long dress and a men's suit jacket over her shoulders.

"They seem to know her", Boone said to the man next to him, still getting warmth from the fire.

"She comes every day with food for us." The man replied.

With her cart now fully at the camp, she opened it up and pulled out paper plates of food for the men and women who lined up next to her. It was an unusual sight of obedience from the people; unusually calm and welcoming to the outside world, which she now presented. Boone watched as she smiled sympathetically to each person, calling them by their names and asking how they were doing and if they needed anything. Every now and then, she would pull out a notepad and write something down, nodding at the person explaining what they needed.

Boone didn't get up as he didn't want to bring attention to himself. The police still lined the tracks and although it would be nearly impossible to pick Boone out of a lineup of the homeless, he didn't want to risk it.

Once the red-headed girl had handed out all the plates, she looked around, stopping at tents and taking notes. She got within one metre of Boone and he noticed that her notepad was scribbled with notes which read: Blanket (Barney, Joe, Harold), bandages (George), Doctor (Elsbeth). She was taking note of what the people needed.

The girl was only a couple of metres away from Boone when she turned around and looked at him.

"Hello", she said, a beautiful smile on her face. "I haven't seen you here before."

"Good morning", Boone said, trying to mirror the friendly look. "I'm just stopping by temporarily. A short stay during my travels."

The girl nodded. "Do you need anything? Extra food, blankets, medicine... books?"

Boone smiled again. "That is very kind of you. I would love a blanket."

The girl wrote down 'blanket' on her list and asked for his name.

"Oh, Boone", he replied.

"Well, thank you, Mr Boone; it's a pleasure to meet you." She reached out her hand to shake his.

Boone stood up now to show her respect, reached out his hand and took hers in it. A tickling flow of energy came through from the girl to Boone. He looked at her with shock on his face.

"Who are you?" he asked now in wonder.

She smiled again. "My name is Mary-Ann."

Chapter Eight

"It's a pleasure to meet you, Mary-Ann."

Boone whirled around thoughts in his mind about her. He could feel that she was different. She was able to tether souls, like him, but wasn't sure if she knew. The energy that flowed off her was light, almost non-existent, almost as though she's gone through life without knowing anything about the afterlife.

She walked away, carrying on her inspections of the shelters, writing her notes still as she poked her fingers through holes in blankets or jackets.

She's either a soul tether, or... a Soul Keeper... but doesn't know it yet. Boone thought to himself.

Boone had almost completely forgotten about the low vibration of death coming from the camp. It wasn't until the two thoughts crossed paths.

This is her first Keep...

Boone took off his beanie, almost like he needed the extra thinking space for what he should do. He looked back at the police, knowing that any alert, such as a scream or fast-paced moment, could make them come over and take a second look at the camp.

He sat back down on the wooden crate, took one last glimpse at Mary-Ann and closed his eyes.

A ringing silence came over Boone and the inside of his mind turned white, turning on and then off, almost like the flash of a camera. He opened his eyes to the world around him once more. He stood up and watched as Mary-Ann continued around the shelters one after the other. This time, Boone could see a white glow illuminating from a tent only a few paces away from where she was going to be.

Mary-Ann smiled as she said goodbye to one woman in rags and moved onto the glowing tent.

"Hello, Charles, are you in there?" She said, making a knocking noise out of the side of her mouth, pretending like she was knocking on a door.

Charles poked only his head and shoulders out, as he looked suspiciously from side to side, almost like a cartoon villain from the papers. She touched his shoulder as a loud, angry voice came from the other side of the camp.

"I knew you were here!" a man yelled. "You bastard!"

The man sprinted from one side of the camp to the other, not caring about any of the other people or their personal items. He knocked over a half-cut metal drum, which had been used as a stool for the fire pit. Within ten paces of Charles, he pulled a metal object from his jacket and held it above his head as he ran. Charles yelled repeatedly at the man to stop. He quickly got onto his feet and put out his arms in front of him with his palms facing the angry man.

Without a second of hesitation, the man lunged forward and drove the metal object into Charles' chest and right into his heart. Mary-Ann screamed a frightful wail as she stepped back, covering her mouth to not draw attention to herself. Charles held the metal object. It still pierced through his chest, a look of shock covering his entire face as the blood trickled down the front of his jacket. He staggered forward and back before finally falling forward completely, driving the object further into him. He was dead.

The man who had just killed Charles looked around at the camp, an evil, angry expression still on his face as others started to scream and run away.

Boone looked over and saw that the police were practically inside the camp now, after hearing all the commotion going on. They stopped about eight shelters away from the man, yelling at him now and telling him to get down on the ground. They held their billy clubs in one hand but were trembling at the size of the man.

He was tall, almost seven feet, with broad shoulders and a big, square head. He almost looked like he could have been part of some kind of super mutant experiment gone wrong.

The man yelled at the police, making them cower and step back further away from him. He looked around and saw that everyone was stepping away or hiding in their own shelters. Mary-

Ann still stood close, unsure of what to do as her hands still covered her face, but now her eyes too. He grabbed her jacket she was wearing and lifted her up, showing her feet dangling in the air as he yelled at the police that he would kill her.

Before anyone could react, he threw Mary-Ann towards the fire. Her body flew through the air almost six paces before her neck landed on the upturned metal drum, leaving a large, blood-gushing wound in her neck.

Boone walked over to her and cupped the side of her face with his hand. They both looked at each other. Mary-Ann, with a sense of dying desperation and Boone, with a look of anger.

"I won't let this happen."

Boone shut his eyes.

A flash of white lightning crossed his vision again as he opened his eyes. He was sitting at the campfire, warming his hands. He turned around and saw Mary-Ann again, smiling.

Boone stood up and started walking towards Mary-Ann as she said goodbye to the previous woman. Just before getting to Charles' shelter, Boone put his hand on her shoulder from behind.

She turned and looked at Boone, a smile still spread across her face.

Being a Soul Keeper, especially a new one, can be tricky. There are certain instances that are created by those who choose the Soul Keepers. In these instances, Boone felt, always had a preferred desired outcome. He had known from years of doing this that this exact point in time was meant to happen. Mary-Ann wasn't meant to die; she was meant to be saved by him. Of course, there were little hints of this too. There was no white glow around Mary-

Ann, no vibrations, hums or ripples. To Boone, this was a clear sign that she was never meant to die. Mary-Ann, however, was too young to even save herself.

"Hello, Mary-Ann", he said.

"Hello, Boone", she replied.

A small but stretched out silence lingered between them both. The smile on Mary-Ann's face not fading one bit.

"My name is Boethius; I am your guide."

Chapter Nine

Confusion crossed Mary-Ann's face as she looked at a serious-looking Boone. She was used to dealing with people whose brains had betrayed them over time, so she wasn't against thinking that he had gone crazy. But the look on his face told her otherwise.

Boone spoke again. "Carry on, but I am here."

She slowly turned her head away, but her eyes didn't follow until the very last moment. Boone stepped back and watched as she called out for Charles.

"Charles, it's Mary-Ann. Knock-knock."

Once again, Charles brought his head and shoulders through the slip in his makeshift tent, eyeing the surrounding camp. Mary-Ann put a hand on his shoulder and just as before, heard the yelling of the big man behind her. This time, however, Boone quickly alerted Mary-Ann to the oncoming man and directed her away from them, putting himself between the two men and her.

This was trouble for Boone, because he could already see down the rail tracks that the police had heard the yelling and were running this way.

Within seconds, Charles had been stabbed in the chest and now lay dying, a light red blood trickled from his chest onto the dirt ground. The police once again yelled at the man to get down on the ground himself before he looked around and couldn't see any other way out than to run.

He bolted to the left and jumped over some people lying low off to the side, trying to avoid the conflict. The policemen followed suit and ran after the man, while one stayed behind to get everyone's statement on the whole situation.

Mary-Ann stood, her hands covering her mouth and eyes as she didn't want to look at what was now lying right in front of her. Boone looked up and saw the policeman coming towards them both, then looked at Mary-Ann. He grabbed her by the shoulders and slightly leaned down towards her.

"Look, I'm sorry to do this to you so fast, but I have to go. I can't have the police see me or know who I am." He looked at the police one last time.

"You can call me Boone or Boethius. I am a Soul Keeper and your guide. You are also a Soul Keeper; you help the dying on their final path. Your life is about to change. I cannot help you right now. When you touched Charles, you would have felt something surge in you and you know it; that was a soul. Take care of him until his final resting place."

He waited, looking into her eyes, trying to work out if she was taking any of this on board. He sighed and glanced around, looking for a way out. He once again cupped the side of her face as a sign of affection.

"I will find you, Mathētēs."

Boone ran. He jumped over the makeshift homes and bounded in the opposite direction that the giant man was running. Looking back, he could see that the police officer didn't know what to do; he was on his own, so he didn't think he should be leaving the scene of the crime, so he didn't.

Boone kept running, but not at an all-out sprint at this point. He regretted having to leave Mary-Ann behind with that secret about herself. She will learn, but not from Boone, not yet.

He jogged west, down streets and between flats and buildings. He slowed to a walk after about ten minutes, figuring this would have given him enough distance between the encampment and himself. Of course, it had only been roughly twelve hours since his escape from Pentonville Prison, so he knew anyone could see him on the streets and alert the police.

With a steady pace and his jacket pulled up and over his ears to cover as much of his face as he could, he kept heading west. He passed Kensington Palace. A memory passed through his mind of a small cottage he helped build for a man named George Coppin in this very spot.

Boone needed to leave not just the city, but the country. He decided he needed to head over the sea, perhaps towards France or Amsterdam. The biggest problem on his mind at this stage was money. On the edge of the street, he spotted a red phone box positioned on the footpath. Walking up to it, he opened the door and shut it behind him. It gave him a small time to just relax, almost like the box didn't have windows all around it. He picked up the receiver.

"Operator" was heard on the other end of the line.

"James Dunlop of Berkeley Court, Marylebone... Please."

The line went silent for a long while as Boone put his head down, hoping Dunlop would pick up.

"Hello?" A woman's voice came from the line.

"Hello?" Boone repeated the greeting back to her. "Maggie?"

The phone went silent for two beats. "Boone, is that you?"

"Yes, Maggie, it's me. Where is James?"

Maggie started to sniff; Boone could hear it come through the line. With an obviously croaky, crying voice, she said, "They've taken him." "Those bastards have sent him to the war. I don't even know where he is."

"When did that happen?"

Boone thought for a moment, trying to think if the police or investigators had pieced together the connection between himself and Dunlop.

"He'll be okay, Maggie, you know he will. I will find him, but it's going to take time for me. I need to get out of the country first and then I will search for him."

This created a problem for Boone. He had initially planned on getting money from Dunlop to purchase a plane ticket out. Now, with him gone, he didn't want to ask Maggie in her emotional state.

Neither of them had problems with money; they both had lifetimes' worth of wealth, but it wasn't always easy to get to. With Boone's planning throughout his whole life, his money was buried deep until he needed it.

He hung up the phone after his goodbyes and started walking again. This time south, trying to get out of the city.

The walk wasn't the issue; it was the fact that now he was walking down roads in regional England, alone. This wouldn't have been much of an issue, apart from the fact that he didn't have crowds to blend into and pretend he was just one of them. If police were to drive by, he knew that they would have pulled over to check his ID. Even if a farmer were to come down the road in a cart, they would have stopped and asked him what he was doing.

Thankfully, after a few more hours of walking, the sun set and the sky turned dark. Each step he took now was completely blind, as the moonlight still hid behind trees for the majority of his trek.

By midnight, Boone had finally reached where he wanted to be. He stood over a small lake in the middle of a wide-open field. The moonlight hit the water as a small amount of wind put small rippling waves across the surface. Boone stripped off his jacket and shirt underneath and laid them both off to the side, near the trunk of a tree. He looked around, making sure no one just so happened to be there watching him and took off his pants and underwear.

Shivering from the now cold winter breeze hitting his body, he headed towards the lake. Putting his foot in, he yelped a small cry and quietly joked to himself that maybe staying in prison would have been better. He slid the remainder of his body into the water and allowed a shield of body warmth to encompass him as he stayed as still as possible. Knowing he wanted to get this over with, he dived under the water.

Boone hit the bottom, his hands running along the bed of the lake looking for something. He surfaced, taking another deep breath of air into his lungs, before plunging into the water once more. Running his hands along the floor again, he felt a large rock, almost in the shape of a starfish. He surfaced once again and once again took another dive. Just off to the side of the starfish rock, he dug with his hands until he hit a wooden object. Grabbing it by its two handles, he pulled it up to the surface and let out a giant breath. He slowly dragged it to the edge of the lake and collapsed over himself, regaining oxygen.

"Should have brought a towel", he said, regretting his choices.

Nevertheless, he put his clothes back over his wet, cold body and immediately felt a hundred times better.

Boone brought the box up further from the water's edge and opened it. A glittering shine bounced from the moon and off the inside contents of the box up to his eyes. It was filled with all sorts of coins, jewels and gold. Even some modern-day pounds.

He took twenty one-pound coins, plus a few other pennies from the top of the box and put them into a small pouch and shut the box again. Taking some twine from the nearest tree and wrapping it around the latch of the box, he let it slip back into the water, pushing it with a large branch as far as he could. This time, it was unmarked and not as well hidden.

The dead of the night provided the benefit of a dark path forward and an easier and less worrisome chance of getting spotted or caught. Unfortunately, it was also still the middle of winter.

The nightly temperature dropped and with Boone's shivering body from the cold water, he couldn't afford to stop. He needed to start walking immediately and get his body temperature back up. If it were the middle of summer, he could have curled up beneath the tree and slept, waiting for the sun to rise.

Boone headed completely north, passing through farmlands and across roads. The path was mostly flat, so the progress was fast. Within six hours, he reached the outer perimeter of Croydon Airport.

The airport was in the middle of nowhere, but the entrance to the building was grand and felt welcoming only to the elite of the time. Boone looked down at himself. The dirty, stained slacks, the jacket with holes in it and the beanie which covered his unwashed and unbathed hair didn't exactly scream elite. He knew that within one second of the workers seeing him, they would know he didn't belong there. Boone kicked himself for not thinking of this sooner.

He put the idea of travelling to the side for now and continued walking past the airport for another forty-five minutes until he reached a small set of shops. One of them had a sign that read, 'S. Adam - Men's Apparel' and had suit jackets on mannequins in the window front. A small bell rang as Boone stepped into the shop. He was acutely aware of how he was going to look to the storekeeper.

"Good morning, Sir!" the man said, looking Boone directly in the eyes, not taking the rest of him in.

"Good morning. I'm looking to travel and need a new suit."

"Excellent!" the man said. "My name is Stuart." He reached out his hand and shook Boone's without any sense of judgment.

Stuart was friendly. He was slightly taller than Boone, bordering on roughly six feet. Slim-waisted and with slightly thinner hair. When he smiled, the crow's feet around his eyes accentuated his genuine personality.

He had Boone immediately step up onto a small plinth and face looking towards a set of three full-length mirrors. Stuart began taking his measurements, running his tape measure along the full length of his arm, down his back and legs and also the circumference of his head. Nodding the whole way, taking mental notes as he went, clearly a master of his own trade.

"Well, Mr Boone", Stuart said, his hand on his chin bringing on a last-minute change in his mind. "I think we can work with you here. Given everything, I think I can get this done for you within three days."

Boone cringed at this. He was desperate to leave the country and didn't have time to wait. He pulled eight of his gold pound coins from his pocket and opened them up to Stuart, placing them into his hand.

Stuart took a step backward in shock. In 1939, the one-pound coins were legal tender, but they definitely weren't in circulation anymore. The coins were gold sovereigns and showed wealth and power to those who held or traded with them.

"Sir, I..." He paused, "Your suit would not be worth as much as this."

"I understand. I need the suit by tomorrow", Boone said.

Stuart looked between the coins and Boone. "Of course, absolutely."

Boone considered for a moment, then pulled out the remaining twelve coins from his pocket, safely in the fabric pouch they were in and handed them to Stuart.

"I need this changed into banknotes. You take your eight; I need twelve back."

If Stuart looked shocked before, he now looked aghast, unsure of what to say.

"But, sir, I, uh...", Stuart stuttered.

"Stuart, I trust you to do the right thing. I know you don't trust the banks, so you won't be questioned when you trade those for notes to whoever you normally trade with. I just need the notes to leave the country."

Stuart tried to push the coins back towards Boone and a scared look appeared on his face.

"How could you possibly know that?" Stuart asked, but Boone refused to accept the coins back.

"I walked into your shop and I saw your ledger open. Unless you only sell one piece per month, I'd say you're not recording everything you do sell. The tin at the top of your shelf behind the counter has marked lines where you are constantly taking down the heavy tin every day. I assume that is where you keep most of your cash."

Boone stepped down from the plinth and walked over to a seemingly random section of the store and tapped his foot.

"Your flooring squeaks here differently than anywhere else, which tells me that you have some kind of underground storage room or tunnel running below. I assume some kind of trade market... Here's the thing, Mr Adam, I'm not any authority, I am not here to 'take you down', but I need someone like you, with your skills."

They both stared at each other, waiting for another ball to drop or questions to flow. It didn't.

Stuart's smile came back onto his face. "Your suit will be ready tomorrow. I will have your twelve pounds in notes ready by nine in the morning. Thank you, Mr Boone."

"Thank you, Stuart. One other thing..." Boone pointed to Stuart's wrist. "I need your watch."

Boone exited the shop, hoping that he could, in fact, trust Stuart to do the right thing by not only getting the suit for him by tomorrow but also not running off with his money. He looked down at his watch and back up; it was still only early in the day. He had to keep out of the street and away from any prying eyes. Boone walked down the road for a few minutes and turned right into a small overgrown garden and leaned up against a tree and slid down to the ground. Closing his eyes, he fell asleep.

Chapter Ten

Boone woke up with a pain in his stomach. A familiar groan sounded from his body, reminding him that he hadn't eaten in the last couple of days. The escape and being out of sight had taken a front seat and hadn't even thought about food until now. He looked at his watch, which had just skipped one in the afternoon.

I need food, he thought to himself.

Walking back onto the same street as the tailors, just opposite it, he spotted a small sign with a green arrow pointing toward the door. The sign read, 'Marge's', with a set of cutlery next to it.

He opened the shop door and paused. Inside looked like something he had seen in the Americas only a couple of decades back. Polished counters, warm lighting and a light crackling radio playing in the background gave off just the right homely vibes. It gave Boone a nostalgic feeling as a woman, perhaps in her sixties or seventies, walked towards him, like she'd been expecting him there all day. The name tag on her apron read, Marge.

"Hello, dearie. Table for one, is it?" The older woman asked.

She pointed towards a small table perched up alongside the front window, where Boone gladly accepted and went to sit down. For a split second, he thought about it being a bad location to get seen, but with the darkened day, not much would be seen through the actual glass.

Boone ordered the bacon and eggs with a side of toast and a hot English tea. Five minutes later, it was set in front of him by the same smiling waitress.

Another five minutes went by and Boone had scoffed down every last crumb on the plate with a slight temptation to lick the plate of the fallen egg yolk. He sat back, feeling a small amount of energy return to him after the two hectic days he had endured. He had barely a moment to even think about the escape and running for his life. Sitting in that cafe, thoughts started to flow about Mary-Ann, hoping that whatever was going on in her head at that very moment wasn't going to damage her too much. So much information might have seemed like complete gibberish to her at the start, but she would eventually put two and two together.

The waitress appeared out of the corner of Boone's eye, caught while in a daydream.

"All done, dearie? Another cuppa?"

"No, thank you; that was delicious." He handed her ten pence. "Keep the change."

"Thank you, love, very kind of you." She replied.

"Say, do you know anywhere that I might find a bed for the night in the local area?"

She did in fact know where Boone could find somewhere to sleep. She told him about a house and gave him directions to where a young lady lived and was renting out a room while her husband had been sent off to the war.

Boone stood up from the table, pushed his chair in, turned to the waitress, and gave her a tip of his non-existent hat. He turned back around and looked out the window across the street. Heading into S. Adam's, there were four police officers, filing in, one after the other. He ducked slightly in the cafe, almost like that would have made a difference to where he was actually standing. Then moved off to the side, so that a set of flowers was blocking anyone's view.

He didn't want to make it obvious that he was watching what was happening across the road, so he decided it would still be best to exit. He moved toward the door and opened it inward. Putting his head down as low as he could, he quickly exited and moved left down the street at a fast pace. By now, the police officers were inside the shop, so unless they were looking out, he bet he was free and clear. He carried on walking at a fast pace down the street and took the first street left.

He walked towards where Marge had directed him and knocked on the door of a two-story brick home. A young lady answered and eventually Boone was shown to a small room with a single bed in it.

Perfect, he thought and lay down on the bed.

It was the softest thing he had rested on in weeks. He sank into the mattress, its edges curled around him like a backwards hug. The sheets and blankets smelled like flowers as they wafted into his nose. He felt like this was his own little heaven. If it weren't for the thoughts of the policemen at Stuart's store, he figured he could have fallen asleep instantly.

The afternoon trickled away, minute after minute, as Boone lay there and thought the plan through in his mind. His biggest concern now was the suit. If Stuart had called the police or told the police anything, he could say goodbye to the suit and the money, with the added bonus of being back to square one. He didn't mind so much about the money going missing, but didn't want to have to spend another day walking back to the lake and fishing out the box again.

Night came easily. Once the sun had set, Boone allowed himself to close his eyes once more and go to sleep.

He woke to a knock at his bedroom door and a small, quiet voice from the landlady.

"Excuse me, sir, would you like breakfast? It's eight am." She said.

"No, thank you though", Boone said in a deep voice after a long fourteen-hour sleep.

Taking a few minutes to clear his head, he inched his way out of bed, put back on his dirty clothing and left the brick house. The food, the sleep and the hospitality were all things that Boone cherished during these last twenty-four hours. It was something he hadn't had since the day of his arrest for the murders. The day he had almost died.

ﻬ

That day started off like any other for Boone. To say it was a usual day for just anyone was an understatement; after all, he was still a Soul Keeper.

It was the 13th of November 1939 - Boone had woken up slightly earlier than normal to a low humming vibration which penetrated through his entire head. Sitting up in his bed, he scrunched his brows together, trying to gauge timeframes and details.

Boone sensed four people, two older and two younger. Death was roughly two pm that day, roughly seven hours from that point.

The timeframe was interesting; it was longer than standard, but not unheard of. The four people dying at once was also above average, in the sense that this was not a health-related death but could have been anything from a house fire to murder. In any case, the details alone were enough to use foresight to check for any unknowns or dangers.

Boone went about his day. He went on his morning walk to the park, plotted away in his back garden, had lunch with a friend and did some regular housework. Once one pm came around, he called for a taxi and headed to Soho Square Garden, which was a couple of blocks away from where he really needed to be, on Wrenford Street.

Boone exited the taxi and walked into the gardens. It was quiet and calming, with flower beds and hedges surrounding the entire garden, making it feel like it was closing you off from the busy streets of the world. He sat down on one of the bench seats next to an older lady who was nose deep in a book. Closing his eyes, he let his senses drift away, one by one.

He opened his eyes and the sky was grey, shaking from what felt like an earthquake taking over the whole of London. He looked sideways at the woman on the park bench, whose eyes still remained on the book in her hands. He felt a tug of emotions pulling him out of his seat and towards Wrenford Street.

The walk only took five minutes and Boone was still roughly thirty minutes early for the deaths. He looked over the building to see if there was anything that could indicate an accident was about to happen, but saw nothing. The building was old, but not ancient. It was a two-story building, built with bricks and had wood-panelled windows. On the top floor of the flat, he could see a glow shining through the windows into the foggy atmosphere.

He looked behind him and saw that there was a small alleyway just behind a medical practice on the corner of the street. He walked back, leaned his body against the building and waited for the event to occur.

Twenty-five minutes later, he saw a man approach the building, but there was something off about him. He had a smile on his face but seemed to walk with purpose. His back was straight and his boots were polished to a shine that most wouldn't have spent time on. Boone couldn't quite put his finger on what was setting him off about this man, but didn't interfere.

Checking his watch, he could see that the deaths would happen any minute now. He walked to the building and climbed the staircase to the top floor and faced the door to the flat. He heard screams and yelling, the kind that only come from someone with a real life-threatening fear. The little girl and boy who were inside wailed, a cry so loud you just knew that they had just witnessed something happening to their parents that they could never unsee.

Then... nothing. The floor was silent; heavy boots were heard running towards the door, which opened and Boone was face to face with the walking man. Boone closed his eyes.

His senses came rushing back to him in the real world and he opened his eyes. Looking to his left, he saw the older woman still sitting next to him, still nose deep in her book. He hated these deaths; he hated the pain he heard and the cries. The adults he could almost deal with, but not kids.

He spent decades of his early life trying to save kids, to change circumstances or to change their fate in one way or another, but nothing ever worked. When he believed in the gods back then, he would curse them for the choices they made and swear against them. Now, he knew he couldn't change anything; he had to let them die no matter what.

Boone stood up once more from the bench seat and walked towards the flat on Wrenford Street. Before exiting the garden, he turned back to look at the woman who he had been sitting next to. She was staring right at him, no longer a face in a book. He smiled and she returned the gesture.

Within only a few minutes, he was back, standing outside the flat block, annoyed with himself that he hadn't given himself more time. He quickly jogged up the stairs of the flat and knocked on the door. A young mother answered it. She looked to be in her mid-thirties, rubbing her hands together to clear them of flour from a dough she was kneading in the kitchen. Boone pretended to know her and held her shoulder, a gentle smile resting across his face.

"Is he in?" Is all Boone asked.

"John? Yes, he's here", She replied.

John came to the door and Boone reached out with a bold smile on his face, inviting a handshake, which John gladly accepted.

"Hi John, my name is Albert. I am an enumerator for His Majesty the King and we are doing census data collection. Are your children home also?"

With that, the children came into view in the room and came straight to the door, saving John from having to answer Boone's question. Boone saw them and gave them both a smile. He bent down and ruffled the heads of both children.

With the soul collection accomplished, Boone's tone lowered and it got softer. "My apologies to your family. I seem to have the wrong address." He said with a smile. "You have lovely children. I wish you all the best."

With that, John closed the door and Boone started to turn around to leave. He immediately recognised the heavy footsteps of the walking man entering the building. Boone didn't panic, but he hurried to the other side of the stairs and crouched down to avoid being seen.

The man reached the top of the stairs and waited at the doorway, not yet knocking. He ran his hands down his jacket, almost like he was clearing out its wrinkles, trying to look as nice as possible. He then reached into the side of his pants. Coming out of his belt buckle was a large ten-inch blade with a black hilt on it.

Boone sighed, now knowing mostly how the whole family dies. The man raised his hand and went to knock on the door. He pulled his hand back and was about to swing when Boone's boots squeaked on the tile floor just behind him. The man turned instantly and looked Boone in the eye. The face, which seemed to have a happy smile on it, was now an untrusting, evil smile. The man immediately ran towards Boone and pounced on him. Boone went down easily, with the man tumbling over him. The man reached back and slammed his fist into Boone's nose as his eyes shot into the back of his head, knocking him semi-unconscious.

The man dragged Boone to the doorway of the flat, knocked on the door and waited. He had his knife back in his hand and was facing it towards the door, waiting for it to open. As soon as it opened, John was standing there and had the knife plunge into his throat, showering the man and Boone with John's blood. John's eyes flew wide and his mouth fell open. He stepped back three paces, attempting to grab whatever was in his throat, but the man had already taken the knife back out. He breathed in with a gurgle as the blood entered his lungs and the lights in his eyes faded.

At that point, the lady of the house came into the room and saw John lying on the ground, surrounded by blood. She let out her own blood-curdling scream before the man put an end to that by knocking her out with his fist. She flew backwards into the edge of a doorframe and fell to the ground. The walking man came back into the hallway of the flat and grabbed Boone by the scruff of his neck, pulling him inside and closing the door behind him.

He pointed the knife at Boone's face before moving it down his body and leaving the tip of it idling on his breastbone, just below the heart. The man, with eyes on Boones, the man slowly inserted the blade through his chest until there was no more blade to be seen. He twisted the knife back and forth as Boone spat up blood from his mouth and nose. The man pulled the knife out in one solid motion, collapsing Boone's left lung in the process.

The man turned back towards the woman and ran the knife across her throat, killing her instantly. The children hadn't seen the deaths of their parents this time because of Boone's interference, but the man looked like he already knew they would have been in their rooms. He entered the boy's room, who asked in confusion who he was, before the voice was cut short. The man then moved onto the girl's room, leaving her in much the same way.

The man came back to the main entrance of the flat and looked at Boone from above. He smiled but said nothing. Boone looked him over, his eyes trailing from the top of his head, down his body and stopping at his open jacket. A glint of silver could be seen coming out from the inside of his jacket pocket. Boone knew exactly what this was, as he had seen it a thousand times before on Dunlop. The man was a police officer.

Without a second to spare, the man reached down and slid his knife across Boone's throat, leaving an open, deadly gash from one side to the next. Boone shut his eyes immediately and heard the man run from the building.

Boone knew he had to be fast; otherwise, this would be the end for him. He focused himself, trying to clear out everything around him. The cold breeze, the slamming of doors from nearby flats and the birds chirping in the trees outside were all dancing through his mind.

Boone focused until his world went white and found himself standing in a wide open room with a glow radiating from it. A lake formed in the middle of the room and Boone walked over to it and peered into the water. He could see himself, the cut along his neckline and the wound in his chest. Calm flowed through him; he knew he needed to heal. He knelt down next to the water, scooped it into his hands and drank from it. The water went down his throat and entered his chest. He looked down and saw that the wound was healing almost instantly. The dark pit that existed from the knife was now getting shallower as the healing worked its way up and onto the skin. The hole closed over and Boone ran his fingers over it, almost like he was feeling his skin for the very first time.

He reached for the water again, putting both hands into the lake and bringing them out, placing them both on his neck as he felt the healing process rapidly spawn new life under his hands. He waited for the feeling of life to come back into his body before leaning over the lake one more time and seeing his complete self looking back.

Within an instant, the lake drained like bathtub water going down into the pipes. The white glowing room around him began to shake and collapse on itself.

Boone opened his eyes and he was back. He was lying on the floor of the flat, completely covered in blood. His hands immediately went to his throat and then his chest. He was completely healed but fully drained of energy. He continued to lie on the ground for a few minutes, completely unable to move his legs or upper torso until he gained the right momentum.

Standing up, he looked around the room and hated what he saw. He swore under his breath that he would get the man who had done this. Suddenly, the sound of police bells could be heard getting closer to the location. Boone knew he had to get out of there and fast. With all his strength and energy, he ran out of the flat and down the stairs. Exiting the building, he immediately ran into three police cars with the red and blue lights still turning on their roofs.

Almost like they'd seen a ghost, the police just stared at Boone as he stared back at them. They immediately reached for the pistols and pointed them at him, telling him to get on the ground and not to move. Almost as though it was within seconds, one of the officers went upstairs, saw the bodies and came back down to label Boone as the killer.

The police forcefully pinned Boone to the ground and handcuffed him. Digging through his pockets, they pulled out ID papers.

Looking at the paper, then back at Boone, he said. "Beau Wainwright. You are under arrest for murder."

৵

Since that very day, this was the first time that made him feel like he was back to his regular life. With a belly full, a clear head and a night of sleep, he was off again.

Chapter Eleven

Boone had left the stone, brick house and was on his way back to the S. Adam's tailor. He didn't want to be too hasty in getting there, as the first thing that was on his mind was the police he had last seen going into the store. The thought of the police setting up some kind of elaborate trap crossed his mind. The idea of him getting to the shop, suiting up and heading to the airport just to be caught ten steps away. It almost made Boone turn around and walk the other way. He didn't. He planned on doing some reconnaissance work from nearby, so he slowed as he got within sight of it at the end of the road.

The road was clear, which again gave Boone a tinge of suspicion, thinking the worst. On the other hand, he did wonder if his mind was playing tricks on him. It wouldn't be the first time that someone had tried both successfully and unsuccessfully to set him up and trap him.

The road had a row of shops on it, about ten going down either side. It started with retail clothing shops, including S. Adam's on one side and the other had food, butchers and Marge's on the other. He didn't want to risk going back to Marge's, as that was far too close to the tailors for him to be comfortable with.

Only two doors down from Marge's was what looked like a bookshop. It didn't have a sign out the front, but the green framed windows perfectly centred the rows and rows of books that could be seen from the outside. Boone wandered down towards the shop, keeping his eyes on the tailors and possible escape routes as he walked.

A bell chimed at the top of the door as Boone swung the door open to the small, dusty bookstore. It was empty but looked like it had several lifetimes worth of living in it. Something about it gave Boone a small sense of nostalgia as he looked around at the countless shelves of books stacked from floor to ceiling. He walked in a few steps more, but still no one came out from the back. Looking behind the counter, he didn't see anyone so continued into the store.

To the right, nestled up against the window was a large brown reading chair next to an open fire and soft sheep rug, making this a perfect vantage point for monitoring Adam's.

Just as the thought of sitting down crossed Boone's mind, he heard a pattering coming from out the back. Less than a second later, a large brown and grey Irish Wolfhound came out and looked at Boone. With a small gruff from him, he went and sat down near the fire and curled himself into as tight of a ball as he could.

"Hello", Boone said to the dog. He didn't respond.

"Hello to you", a voice bellowed out.

A young, lean, red-haired man had appeared from behind a curtain at the back of the store. Even from just those few words, 'hello to you', Boone could hear the accent of an Irishman. Even without the accent, one look at his Celtic tattoos would have told anyone the same.

"Just having a wander, are we? Or is there something in particular you're hoping to find?" The red-haired bookkeeper asked.

Oh, you know, just trying to escape from the cops, using your bookstore as a hideout.* Boone thought to himself.

"Just hoping to purchase a couple of books and sit down to read them?" Boone said, positioning it as a question to see if the bookkeeper would mind.

"Absolutely, grab a book, park yourself in front of the fire and stay as long as you like." The man replied to him.

With that, he walked towards the first bookshelf, moving his head around as his eyes lapsed over every spine trying to find something he hadn't read before. Most of the books were old, some of which even dated back hundreds of years but still looked to be taken care of on the shelf.

Boone's eyes grew wide as he noticed one book in particular. It was old, roughly 200 years, dusty and didn't look like it had been opened in almost just as long. It was titled: The Herbal Lore of the Highlands, written by Sorcha MacKinnon. Boone smiled as he opened the book, hearing the cracking of the spine as it opened. He turned to the front page and saw all the way at the bottom of the page it read.

'To my love, my one and only, Boethius Boone.'

A small tear appeared in the corner of Boone's eye as he read it over and over again. He closed the book and placed his hand firmly on the front cover.

I love you.

He smiled and took the book over to the reading chair next to the fire and opened it up.

Boone would have loved to have actually read the book as it had been decade upon decade since he had even read anything by Sorcha. Unfortunately, he had other things that he needed to keep at the forefront of his mind, most importantly, his life and not getting caught.

From the reading chair, he had a perfectly framed view of Adam's Tailors in his vision. He sat, book in lap, watching and waiting.

Hours flew by without a single person entering or exiting not only this bookstore, but the tailor's as well. The bookkeeper didn't look towards Boone at all during this time, which made him feel at ease about being there for so long. He did however, bring over a tea and a couple of biscuits at lunchtime. He sat them down on the side table and walked away without saying a word.

Another couple of hours passed and Boone looked at his watch. It was nearing three pm and so far there was no sign of any police. Nothing suspicious or worrying had happened, so he figured he would make a move for the shop.

Boone hopped out of his chair and went to the front counter with the book and placed it on the glass shelf next to the register.

"I'd like this one, please."

The young bookkeeper looked from the book to Boone. He picked it up and put it into a brown paper bag. He held the book out to Boone.

"From the look on your face, I believe this book is yours anyway."

Boone eyed the man and his features. "This book is over 200 years old. What makes you say that?"

The bookkeeper smiled and kept the book hovering between them as he tried to hand it over.

Boone looked at him through slitted eyes and closed off a few of his senses, trying to gauge anything from the man. He couldn't sense anything. This man, as far as Boone was aware, was normal.

"Thank you." Boone said as he reached out gingerly for the book, graciously accepting the gift.

He tucked the book under his arm and exited the shop, heading towards the tailor's.

Once again, Boone pulled his collar up against the side of his head, trying to get as much cover as he could to hide his face. He kept looking around at different shops and down the sides of alleyways as he got closer and closer to the tailor's, but there was nothing.

He opened the door and the bell above him rang. Stuart looked up from his work and his eyes flew open.

"Mr Boone, you're back! Quickly come in."

Boone shut the door behind him, eyeing the road he had just left. He walked over to Stuart who held a large brown envelope on his desk.

"Mr Boone, the police are after you and will be here soon. I have your money and your suit." He pulled out the banknotes, counting them out.

Pulling out a small blue passport, he handed it to Boone. "I also got you this... Mr MacNab."

Boone took the passport and opened it up. It had the name 'Grant MacNab' on it, with a blank space for a photo.

"What is this?" Boone asked.

"This, sir, is your only way out of this country. I assume that is why you are leaving. I had the police here asking questions. As they were leaving, there was a woman who I noticed was hanging about close by. I kept an eye on her for a while until she finally crossed the road and came in. She left me a note, which mentioned you were framed for murder and that I can trust you. Which, strangely enough it seems we had already trusted each other."

"You caught me out sir, you knew exactly who I was and what I was doing." Stuart walked over to the square of ground that Boone had tapped the previous day. "This... is exactly what I am doing."

He reached down and pulled up the floor below, showing a staircase that ran down into an underground basement, hidden from any other entry. They walked down and Stuart pointed Boone to a small room off to the side to get changed. Boone headed in and slipped on his new suit, which fit perfectly.

"Go stand over there", Stuart said, pointing to a spot in front of a white background. He pulled up a camera and shot.

Five minutes later, Boone had a picture on his new passport and barely knew what to say. Rarely did he put trust in someone that he didn't know. Stuart had mistaken the fact that Boone had given him so much money for trust. Reality was, the money wasn't important to Boone; it was just another thing he had to overcome to leave the country. But now, he could see that Stuart was perhaps more than he originally let on, or at least more than Boone could see.

"It's 3:10pm Sir, you must go." Stuart ushered Boone back to the main floor of the shop.

With a solid handshake between the two, Boone left the shop and started walking toward the airport once more. He felt like a new man, back in clothes he at least felt comfortable in. Something that people wouldn't give him a second look as he walked down the road. The fedora also helped peering eyes from seeing who he really was.

The walk back to the airport was uneventful, but still put Boone on edge and he let out a sigh of relief once he stepped into the circular driveway of the airport entry.

The entry was grand, with a stone arch that curved over the top of the main terminal. A countless number of cars would pull in, a doorman would come to the vehicle and open the door for the man or woman who was travelling that day. It was the royal treatment and travelling by air was not something just anyone would be doing.

Boone kept walking along the footpath which lead to the entry and the two doormen. They both eyed him off with slight suspicion. Or at least that is what Boone felt. He did just walk in from seemingly nowhere, with no vehicle and a very expensive Italian suit. Nevertheless, they tipped their caps at him as he shuffled past and into the terminal.

It had been at least a decade since Boone had travelled by air and even then; it had only been a handful of times in his life. He had travelled to the far reaches of the world, but in most cases had taken boats or transport ships onto which he could pay refuge. So, with this flight, he still considered it to be a risk. Something about falling eight thousand feet at high speed to their death was one way to completely wipe out a Keeper, giving no time to heal.

Boone walked towards the main check-in counter, which was positioned near the main entry. He made his way to one of the girls who was working and put on a smile for her. She looked at Boone and gave him a pearly white, toothy smile, which perfectly framed her bright red lips.

"Good evening, sir. Your name?"

"MacNab... Grant MacNab", he replied and put down his passport on the counter.

"I'd like to book your next flight to France, please."

"Certainly, sir, let me check."

She looked down at an opened logbook in front of her. Running her finger down the page, she saw the line which read 'Paris, France' and tapped it.

"You're in luck, sir, we have one more seat heading out this evening at 4:00pm, but this is the latest because of the blackout after dark."

"I'll take it." He said, handing her five one-pound notes. "Is this enough?"

The woman accepted the five pounds and returned him his change. Boone looked around the room, noticing that the airport didn't have any additional security or police than it normally would. He expected at least some. After all it was an airport, but wasn't sure if he was going to have some kind of crowd waiting for him as he entered the terminal.

Boone barely had to wait for the flight. By the time he was done with the girl at the check-in counter, he headed for the boarding area and sat down on one of the plush seats, finding a newspaper laying next to him. He picked it up and held it out in front of him and smack right in the middle of the page; he looked face to face, with himself. He quickly put down the paper so fast it drew the attention of a few of the people around him. Slowly picking up the paper again, but not so high, the news article read, 'Beau Wainright - MURDERER ESCAPES - Hide your children'.

Boone put down the paper, a little of his spirit broken. A long life lived did not circumnavigate the pain he felt as others thought of him as nothing more than a murderer, even worse, a child murderer. He knew that time would forget; he knew that all too well, but he didn't want to run again. His plans were simple: get to France and potentially further into Europe, maybe country side somewhere, spend ten years on the outskirts and then return once the papers were gone and the memories faded. He hoped his memories would fade as well.

A young pimple faced teenager wandered into the waiting area of the terminal asking for attention from everyone.

"Uh, um, passengers for the 4:00 pm flight to Paris, please proceed to the tarmac."

Eleven other people stood up all at the same time, ready for their flight. They all started walking towards the tarmac. Boone put a smile on his face. He was glad to not only be on his way out, but glad he wouldn't have to be constantly on the run, putting his head down everywhere he went.

The plane was a Dragon Rapide, a modern twin-engine biplane with dual wings. It still made Boone happy that technology like this now exists in the world. He shook his head, wondering how on earth it actually flew. As the crowd headed for the tarmac, something was odd. There seemed to be far more crew surrounding the plane than Boone had remembered over the last few years. A whisper came from a couple of ladies just in front of him.

"Why are there so many people here?" One lady said to the other with a cupped hand over her mouth.

"I heard from George that apparently Walter said that they're looking for this Wainwright fellow; they have all airports and train stations covered across the entire country." The other lady said, eyes shot into a look of 'can you believe that?'

Boone slowed as they got closer to the plane. He was now on the tarmac and to just stop now would be completely suspicious to anyone around. He was thinking and thinking and had no other option than to run. He took off his hat and threw it backwards to look like the wind had caught it. He turned and jogged towards it, picked it up... and ran.

Chapter Twelve

Boone ran as fast as he could out of there and didn't look back. If he did, he would have seen eight undercover police officers looking slight dazed and confused at each other before whispers spread amongst them. The questions started to flow as to what they had just seen.

One officer pulled out a photo and showed it to one of the passengers who were still boarding the plane. She nodded a confirmation that the person who ran was the person in the photo. It was, Beau Wainright.

By this stage, in those very few minutes, Boone already had a head start on everyone he left behind. With his heart pumping and mind racing, he didn't stop. The adrenaline that coursed through his veins kept him running with no plans to even consider stopping.

He was hundreds of metres away by now, but Boone was in trouble. Croydon Airport was literally in the middle of nowhere. There were no buildings nearby to sneak behind, no forests to dodge between the trees and there were no fields for him to jump into and hide behind the corn or lie down in the sorghum. He had no other option than to keep running down the same road he was on. The thought played over in his mind that the officers wouldn't be on foot; they would have their own vehicles and would be seconds behind him.

Just as that thought occurred, he heard the sound of an engine bustling its way towards him. He picked up the pace and his legs started to go so numb that he felt like he was running on nothing but clouds. That at any moment, he would just lift off into the sky. It wouldn't be the first time he had wished it, but he wanted some other power than just being a Soul Keeper.

"Give me super speed, god dammit!"

The sound of the car was getting louder and seemed to be just behind him. He split off, taking a right-angle turn into one of the flat, green fields of nothingness. He ran as fast as his legs would take him, carefully avoiding any of the now holy ground from cow or horse's hooves. He got fifty metres away and the car started beeping its horn over and over again. He got one hundred metres away, the vehicle still beeping its horn. Boone risked it and turned his head around to glance. It was Maggie!

Boone couldn't believe his eyes. It wasn't the police at all; it was Maggie who was speeding up behind him, beeping her horn. Boone started once again to run, but this time back towards her. In no time at all he got to the car and she yelled for him to get in, which he did with no hesitation. He looked back towards the airport and a slew of black police vehicles were hot on their heels. Maggie put her foot on the accelerator and they both were pushed into the back of their seats as the car picked up speed.

"I can't have you involved!" Boone yelled.

"Well, I already am! You are the only one who can get my husband home and you are going to do it!"

It dawned on Boone that Maggie wasn't just doing this for him, or for Dunlop. She was doing it for herself. She had stuck around Dunlop through thick and thin; she loved him dearly, even knowing every last secret he ever had, even the ones that Boone didn't even know about. She couldn't imagine spending her life without him and she knew that if Boone went down, there was a high probability that he would too.

They kept driving at that speed down the road as far as the street would get them. Maggie was not an experienced driver; in fact, she had barely any experience at all. Once they got to the end of the road and had to make a turn, Maggie yelled at Boone.

"Your turn!"

Without hesitation, Boone hopped out of the car and ran around to the driver's side and got back in. Maggie had crossed over the centre console of the car and was now on the passenger side. Boone took two seconds, making sure that she was safe and secure, before putting his foot down and going for it.

The car was a Hillman Minx, not the fastest Dunlop could have purchased, but it was solid. It handled the corners well and you knew that it was never going to break down. Especially in a high-speed chase.

The police were in their Wolseleys. Faster paced vehicles overall but they were heavy, took a while to get up to speed and didn't take the corners as easily as the Minx. This is where Boone knew he was going to lose them.

Boone headed for the city where he knew he would duck and weave between the traffic, speed around corners and squeeze down alleyways. He did just that.

He spent the next twenty minutes playing dodgems with other cars in the streets. He outmanoeuvred the police cars with ease and made his way north attempting to exit the town. In a moment of calm and clarity, he slowed down and marked himself as a normal driver in the city.

"How did you find me?" Boone asked.

"I've been in contact with Mr Adam, the tailor, who mentioned that he got you a passport. He said you'd either use it for ID or try to get out of the country. I last spoke to him this morning, so I've been waiting all day. I didn't recognise you when you went into the airport, but when I saw a running man coming out, I knew that had to be you.

"Thank you, Maggie", he said genuinely. "I don't know what I would have done if it weren't for you."

Maggie didn't say anything for a while. They rode in silence as Boone drove the vehicle through the main drag of London. He looked out and saw white posters littering the walls and streetlamps every few hundred metres. He passed a few before something clicked in his head. He slowed to a crawl as he inspected one and kept driving. On the next one, he completely stopped and exited the vehicle and walked straight up to the poster and ripped it off the wall. It was a photo of him, of Beau Wainwright, with a caption that read 'WANTED FOR MURDER'.

Devastation washed over Boone once more as he knew this was going to be a long wait.

Boone went back to the car and bent down to look at Maggie, still in the passenger seat.

"This is me", he said. "I need to leave you here. I need to hide, but I can't leave the city; the souls will just drag me back here."

"What about James?" she asked, her voice cracking slightly.

"I can't get to him, Maggie. I've tried. He's over there somewhere and I will help him. I promise you that. I will keep an eye on him and make sure I can feel him. But I can't get there."

Maggie paused, tears rolling down her cheeks as she wiped them away just as fast.

"If he dies...", Maggie started to say but was cut off by Boone.

"I know, Maggie... He won't die."

She nodded and sniffed up her tears. "The posters went up yesterday. They're all over the city; you have no chance of staying here."

"I have to try."

Boone watched as Maggie drove away, turned a corner and vanished. Next, it was Boone's turn. The heavy weight on his shoulders became lighter as his mental exhaustion overtook him. He gave up.

Part of him wanted to turn himself in and face the execution for the deaths he never committed. The other part of him wanted to not only keep running, but outrun time. He knew and would tell himself over and over again that people would forget. The only difference is, Beau Wainright was him; he was Beau Wainright, or at least he had been for at least the last twenty years. The people who knew him, the friends that he made during that time, the shops he visited and bought bread and milk from. They all knew him now as Beau Wainright... murderer.

Boone stood north of the city, with the lingering uncertainty hanging over his every moment. He looked around but didn't know where to turn for help. He knew one place that would take him in, one place he could blend into the crowd and be forgotten by humanity.

Boone walked back towards the prison, heading for the homeless encampment. He hung onto a slight hope that maybe Mary-Ann was there and, as a Soul Keeper, wouldn't turn him in.

Chapter Thirteen

The first few days of life in the encampment went by slowly. Boone spent most of his time awake, waiting for Mary-Ann to appear at the end of the tracks, pushing the same cart he had seen her with the first time. Being a tramp was as solitary as life could get, but most still had at least the people they surrounded themselves with. Boone still didn't know who he could trust, so he mostly kept to himself.

You would think that someone walking into a camp with a suit on and polished shoes would turn heads, but you'd be wrong. The city of tents provided a large population of drug users and mental health sufferers, which meant they didn't look twice at you. The homeless who were completely coherent were the ones who did notice, but they were also the ones who understood the most. They understood the struggles that people fought to keep food in their mouths and a roof over their heads. They were the ones who knew how hard it was to keep a family or and how easy it was to lose a family. They didn't question Boone and he was glad for it.

The days turned into weeks and the weeks into months. 1940 had ticked on by a couple of months back and the summer was a welcome change to everyone in the camp, being that no one would almost freeze to death. By this stage, Boone had established his own section of the camp, right next to where Charles used to be. It was small, dusty and cold at times, but it was his and he was still alive. After the first month, he opted to lose the suit and trade up for some warmer clothing, which included a long woollen trench coat and a woollen beanie again.

Mary-Ann hadn't been seen again and although Boone now asked people about her, most either chose not to answer or perhaps pretended that she never existed. It didn't stop him from waiting and watching every day alongside his make-shift fireplace. Boone could shut off his senses and feel her energy somewhere in the city but couldn't pinpoint where. There was something strange about that. Normally Boone could find just about anyone as long as they had some kind of connection. Whether that person wanted to let Boone in was another question.

As August started, more of the war was talked about at the camp. People would talk of the phoney war that was constantly brought up from the news. Of course, by now it didn't seem like so much of a phoney war, but a potential threat. Everyone was worried. The streets were emptier as more and more people left the city. The schools were closed and the kids no longer played on the streets or in the parks. It was an eerie feeling, no matter whether you believed in the war or not.

On the seventh of September, Boone woke to a vibrating hum across the entire city. Her was unsure what it was about but knew that no one else around him felt it. With his senses closed off to the world around him, he peeked into the future and saw that the whole of London was going to be shocked by the many lives around the city ending that day.

Boone sat in silence, contemplating the fate of himself and many of those around him. His memories of past wars flashed back into his mind. The Great War. The death and devastation that filled the fields of France where he was stationed was something that he would never forget and not to mention, hoped never to take part in again. He remembered the sleepless days and nights when he would put his life at risk to help transition the souls as he jumped from field to field and side to side, transitioning between speaking French, to English and then to German.

The faces of his squad still plagued his thoughts from that time and he didn't want to see the loss of more of his people. Dunlop refused to talk about it for years, either shutting off completely or simply walking away.

Boone reached for his chest and pulled out a small, round pendant that hung from twisted old twine around his neck. He gripped it tight, a small tear puddling in his eye for the ten Soul Keepers and the millions of humans that were lost.

He wasn't sure what was about to happen in the city but knew it would be bad. There wasn't a place or location that he could go to that he knew for sure would be safe for him to stay and shield himself from any oncoming wave of enemy.

His first instinct was to leave London and head north toward Scotland. However, he knew he had to be down here for the souls to transfer.

Boone looked around the camp and watched people as they got up and out of their shelters, making their way to fires, eating yesterday's dinner or simply just staring into nothingness. He sighed, knowing that this may be the last few hours of these people's lives.

Boone took a pillow and laid it on a clean part of the ground. He sat on it, closed his eyes and wiped away the world around him. He focused, bringing his senses completely closed before a flash of light crossed over his vision.

Years of training, experience and self-meditation had given Boone such a keen sense of his powers that it was easy for him to use his foresight. If anyone were to ask how it was done, such as a new Soul Keeper or loved one. He would describe it as putting one life on hold temporarily to jump into the next. The next life would show him the paths that were about to happen, show him events and tragedies which he knew he couldn't stop or help. After he was done, two things would happen. The last Keep would die and his mind would transport back to the original life on hold, or he would simply bring himself out of it.

Inside foresight, Boone stood up in a half-daze from the shining white glow that covered the city. It was almost like a constant flash of sheet lightning hanging in the skies. His chest felt tight as the pull from so many souls tugged and begged for him to come.

The walk from Islington to the city felt surreal. The blackout was still in full effect, so the streets felt empty and were lined by shadows of buildings rather than the usual people walking to work or school. Most of the glows and pulls that Boone felt were from nearby flats or businesses, rather than those that were on the street.

As he got closer to the city, more people seemed to be walking the streets as they went about their everyday. People still had to work, make money and put food on their tables. So, when it came to staying at home, this wasn't an option for most.

Boone looked at his watch and did his own quick calculation based on pull and vibration through the city. He couldn't quite pinpoint which death would be the first but knew that they would all happen at roughly the same time. He figured this had to be a bombing run by the Germans.

He looked to the sky, almost to see if he could spot any planes overhead already. The fact that so many people would be dying in the city meant that it would be nearly impossible for only a few Soul Keepers to get to them all, especially when they were mostly in their homes.

There was one Soul Keeper that Boone knew would be in the city today. He was a few hundred years old, but no one really knew his real name. They all could feel each other if they needed to. He was known as The Collector. The mystery surrounding The Collector travelled deep into the world of Keepers. So much so that the way he detected and collected souls was a complete unknown to even his closest confidants. Boone knew that The

Collector would detect days earlier than most and then spend that time in between scouring the city, knocking on doors and taking the souls of as many people as he could. Even with this happening, there were still some that were missed.

The day moved on and Boone still roamed the city in Foresight. By now the sun spread across the sky and it was getting towards the afternoon when people would start to knock off work.

At 4:20pm, Boone heard the familiar rumblings of an aeroplane engine rattle across the sky. Within seconds, a warning came across London, a wailing, undulating tone, rising and falling as it screamed out for everyone to get indoors and to safety. Boone watched as people ran for their lives.

Not only hearing the sound but seeing the planes in the distance put a serious feeling in the mix. Businessmen in suits ran to the closest shelters, hands on heads, trying not to lose their hats. Women pulled the hands of the small children doing the exact same thing. They would run for the bus or run into buildings to either get home or hide.

Ten minutes later, the first bomb fell. Boone watched as the first plane flying from above dropped a large payload from the sky and allowed it to soar to the ground. It feeling like it took an hour just to get from the plane to the ground. The memories of the Great War came flooding back once more. In reality, it was only seconds.

It hit within a kilometre of him; the ground shook and the explosion sounded in the distance, but there were no screams, almost like everyone was just thankful it didn't hit them. Boone looked up and knew this was going to be a lot worse than he had ever seen before, as countless planes dropped their loads towards London. Boone stood at one of the city gardens, watching from below. He sighed as one of the bombs came tumbling towards him.

"This... isn't good."

This was all he said as the bomb came closer and closer and hit. The world went dark.Chapter Fourteen

"Wah!"

An unintended cry came from Boone as he fell over from his position back at the camp. A couple of the others that surrounded him looked, barely a sign on their face to say, 'Are you okay?' but nothing came. They all went back to what they had been doing.

Boone sighed as he settled back into his chair. He contemplated going back into his foresight visions, but this was mostly for selfish reasons. Of course, he cared about everyone in the city; it was hard not to. But there was a small, selfish part of him that wanted to know if the site, which he now calls home, survives. Trying to find another place to live wouldn't be hard, but it had its risks.

He looked at his watch.

It's early. The bombs start to drop at roughly half past four... that means around nine hours until the start of it.

He stood up and stretched his back. He held one arm and turned his body so he heard the release of his bones throughout. Twisting the other way, hearing the same.

The months of sleeping on a mostly hard floor had challenged him physically. His body was thirty, but he felt eighty again.

He gathered a few belongings from his tent, making sure to pack a bit of money and his book from Sorcha in a small satchel he had traded for a couple of months back. He looked around at the others in the campsite and wanted to warn them. He didn't know where exactly each bomb would drop, but he assumed everyone had survived from the camp, considering he felt no vibration from them and didn't see any glow from the camp in his foresight. The camp, on the other hand, he wasn't sure about.

Perhaps once the first bombs dropped, everyone ran, abandoning their homes before they were also pulverised into dust.

Boone said his goodbyes to a few of the people around the camp. He wouldn't have called them friends, but they were good people. They had traded and looked after each other when each other needed it. He hoped to see them again.

Boone had nine hours and roughly fifty souls he needed to collect. Based on the vibration pattern, he started walking once again towards the city. The fifty souls were an assumption, or a guess. The guess was an educated one however and Boone knew shouldn't be more than one or two off that number. Fifteen minutes into walking, he slowed. The planning in his head was something he needed to get right. For every soul that needed saved, he only had a limited time to save them and that time was already counting down.

Fifty souls, nine hours. That's five to six souls per hour, which means I need to get to a soul every ten minutes and I'm here just dawdling around!

He shook his head to himself, almost like a disappointed teacher watching a child not doing their schoolwork like they were asked to.

Boone heard a familiar voice coming from one of the flats that he had just passed. He stopped, took two steps back and looked around a bush to see who it was. He saw the back of a head that he did not recognise, but the voice he did. Boone squinted his eyes, almost like that would help with trying to remember who the voice belonged to, but the features didn't.

The man turned around from the flat and came walking down towards Boone and stepped around the bush, coming face to face with him.

"Hello, Boethius", the man said, a slight tired rasp to his voice.

"Hello, Col", Boone replied. "I knew you'd be in the city; I just didn't expect to run into so soon."

"Yes, I'm here in this wonderful time of death and sadness, like always." He said, a slight sarcastic tone from the words.

Col, as Boone called him, was The Collector. Boone knew the burden all too well of collecting souls every day. He also knew that The Collector took ten times the amount of souls that any other Soul Keeper did. The mental exhaustion plagued his face in a face that showed nothing but doom and sorrow. In contrast, Boone was a lot older than Col, but they had taken roughly the same number of souls over both their times.

Boone nodded. "You sound tired... To be expected, I suppose."

Col let out a long sigh, like he'd just gotten off a two-day shift at the coal mine. "I am tired Boe, I think I'm done. I'm retiring."

Again, Boone nodded at this statement. Soul Keepers didn't really have a retirement date or a day where they could just take a sick day. The universe gave them their duties; it told them when to be out there and where to be. But it also helped them when they couldn't. Boone was a great believer in the saying, 'Things happen for a reason.' And it was true, or at least it felt like it was crafted that way. Obviously, human intervention and free will were placed far above what the universe could decide. Meaning that if a Keeper desperately wanted to retire, chances are they would. On those odd times when no one else would be available, they would be called for, as long as they were still alive, of course.

"You're looking old. Are you sure you want to retire now?" Boone questioned Col.

"I haven't healed in fifty years. I'm lucky I'm not dead from cancer at this stage", he said as he coughed unironically. "I have two hundred souls today…"

He left that ending hanging. Boone knew what it meant. The two hundred souls represented life extension, but only if he wanted it. Boone was right, though. The Collector looked old and worn out, so he understood the desire to live a normal life.

Col stuck his arm out towards Boone. Boone looked down at his hand and then at Col. He reached up and shook it. Col turned around and walked away.

"You will see me again, Boethius." He said without looking back.

Boone watched as The Collector walked around the corner and out of sight. Most times, you could tell just by their goodbye whether you would actually see them again. It was a common saying among the Keepers that we would all see each other again in the next life. Of course, no one was really sure of that. They were pretty sure the souls were saved for a reason rather than just nothingness in the afterlife. In any case, Col's goodbye didn't always mean a goodbye forever in this life, but the chances were high.

An elevated vibration turned Boone around to see a woman stepping out of her car, juggling two bags of groceries while searching for her keys in her purse. This was his first keep today and just so happened that she came to him rather than searching her out. This would be an easy one, Boone figured. It meant no knocking on doors and pretending to be who he wasn't.

Boone jogged over to the woman and put on a rather large smile. "Good morning! Let me help you with those!" He searched for the bags before the woman even had a second to think.

"Oh, thank you", she said. Swapping her eyes between her purse and Boone.

They walked up the six steps to her front door and unlocked it. She put the keys back in her purse and Boone handed the bags back to her, slightly brushing up against her hand. He smiled at her one last smile before turning and walking down the steps.

The woman closed the door as he watched from the curb, a smile still on his face.

He waited five heartbeats before turning to his left.

"Hello", he said to her again, but this time it was to her soul.

She looked around in confusion. She had just seen two realities. One was of her outside her flat, watching herself move into her home and the second was from her own eyes in her own body, watching herself shut the door, closing it off from the helpful but strange man outside. She said nothing to Boone, but he knew she was confused.

"It's okay", he said. "I have saved your soul for the afterlife. Your loved ones will be there momentarily. For now, let me guide you through the last remaining hours of your life."

The next few hours were spent much the same way. Boone found the soul he needed to Keep, grabbed it in some way or another and moved on. Eventually, a flock of wandering souls tailed his every move as he gained more and more, like a forever-growing, terrible scoreboard.

As Boone headed down Bedford Place after his last Keep from number seven. He heard a wailing cry coming from the end of the street. It made Boone immediately alert to what may be happening and he stopped in his place, attempting to double check if it was happening outside or inside. The wailing continued and a small "Help me!" followed. Boone ran down the street towards Russell Square, across the road and into the gardens.

The crying and wailing were coming from a woman. She was on the grass, almost in the middle of the square. She was on the ground, her knees and lower legs sat against the grass and her head was tilted down towards the ground as she covered her face with her hands.

Boone could hear the pain in her like it was a pain that was familiar to him. He reached her and felt a flow of energy come from her body.

"Mary-Ann?" he said.

She looked up at Boone with red eyes and tears falling down her face. "Please make it stop! Please!"

Boone knelt down in front of her with only a few centimetres falling between their faces. He grabbed her hands and took them away from her head, placing them on his knees. He reached his hands back up and put them on either side of her face.

"I need you to put complete trust in me. I will help you. I will stop the pain."

He closed his eyes. She was shaking still, knowing that she would do anything at all to help. She followed suit and her eyelids drooped.

Boone immediately closed off all of his senses, sending him into a white open space with no noise, no colours or objects, no up and no down. It was a void. He looked around for Mary-Ann, but she wasn't there yet; she hadn't put her trust in him yet. He hoped she would follow him there as he counted down from ten, reaching zero and then starting again. Before he reached seven, she appeared, almost like she had just phased her body into existence.

Mary-Ann immediately collapsed and pulled herself into a ball while lying sideways on the ground. She had her eyes shut tight, but seemed to be more relaxed than she had been. Boone sat cross-legged on the ground near her, watching as she still lay on the ground, arms around her knees. Nothing but silence hung between them for the next few minutes until she eventually opened her eyes.

"Hello", he said.

"Where am I?" Mary-Ann asked, as her eyes darted around the room of nothingness in an attempt to lock onto something.

"You are nowhere", he responded cryptically. "I'm guessing this feels at least a little better?"

She uncurled herself from her locked arms and slowly stood up, dusting off her legs once she was straightened. She looked down then at her hands.

"No dirt?" She said, part question, part comment.

Boone smiled. It was interesting to see someone in the void for the first time, completely closed off from all senses of the real world. She was taking it in particularly well, considering most freak out if they don't find it themselves. They often feel like some kind of god has taken them to another planet.

"No dirt", Boone replied. "How are you feeling?"

"I feel... sick but... good. Why is it so... nothing?" She asked, with a look on her face almost like she was trying to look into her own brain.

"Mary-Ann, do you remember me?" Boone asked.

"Yes, of course, you said something about being a Soul Keeper and you're my guide and there was something about dying people. I'm sorry, I was in shock at the time and it felt like everything around me was going so fast."

"I understand. I'm sorry I had to give you a lot of information in a very short period of time. I was charged with murders I did not commit." Boone said.

Suddenly, a memory snapped into Mary-Ann's head. "You're the man from those wanted posters." She stepped back. Almost like she was getting ready to run.

"Yes, Mary-Ann, I am a Soul Keeper and so are you. We are here to help take the souls of people who are close to death. We do this to ease their transition between this life and the next. Those people who were murdered were not killed by my hands. I got caught up with the real killer and was in the wrong place at the wrong time."

Mary-Ann stared at Boone, looking him up and down. She examined him and created what felt like her own brief report in her head about what he looked like, what he said and what this room was like. She took one step back towards Boone, almost like she had had a revelation.

"Is that why I feel like this?" she asked.

"You need to tell me how you feel. We're not all the same; most are, but not all."

"That man at the encampment who got killed. I felt like I needed to be there for him and I felt like I failed him when he died." She said, with a look of disappointment crossing her face.

"You actually helped him pass. He got murdered, but he did not feel it as his soul was already in you."

"They said that you'd been going there for months, but you went for him?"

"I did, yes. I had this... feeling like I had to be there and I didn't know why, so I kept going back just for him. I had felt it for years."

"Years? What do you mean by years? Do you feel a pull or a vibration, or a memory or something?"

"Yes!" she screamed, "Like a vibration! But his was louder than most."

Boone thought for a second, unsure of how this would be possible. The feeling of a soul needing help for years was completely unheard of. He then clicked onto what she had just said.

"Louder than most? Is there most?" Boone questioned.

"Oh yes, a lot more. Since my earliest memory as a baby, I've had these weird feelings and this lower drumming, which felt like it went through the air from everywhere around me. It was loud, so loud! But now... it's gone. I feel free. Oh! Also, I get these flashes, like pictures coming up behind my eyes to show me a house or a person or something, but it goes so fast that I can't really see who it is."

Boone and Mary-Ann talked for what felt like hours in the void. In the real world, they still sat, kneeling in the grass, eyes shut, but only seconds had passed.

They talked about her pull towards death and the vibrations and humming. The flashes she felt throughout her whole life seemed to be foresight of events which were about to pass at some point or another. They seemed to pass by so fast she was unable to control them or get any information out of them. From what Boone could put together, she was feeling and sensing the deaths of every single person she would ever Keep. Boone needed help.

"I don't want to leave here. It's so peaceful." Mary-Ann said.

"I will teach you how to come here whenever you need rest. You can even sleep here and it'll repair your mind like regular sleep would. Essentially, allowing your human body to stay awake every day of your life, should you choose. But you need to be strong and have that energy from souls to do that."

Boone carried on, "I need to help understand what you are going through. I'm going to find someone, but it will take time. I need you to go to all the vibrations and humming you feel and take their souls. This is your life now."

They exited the void and the immediate pain that Mary-Ann felt was clear in the expression on her face. Nevertheless, she picked herself up off the ground, gave Boone and hug and walked away without saying another word.

By 3:30 pm that day, Boone had found all the Souls that he needed to Keep. He tuned his senses and looked around at the fifty-two souls that trailed behind him, like baby ducklings following their mother in need of protection. He was in the open and there were people who were still alive around him, but he didn't care if they all heard.

He boomed his voice over the crowd of souls. "Hello! The city will be attacked in a blitz of planes flying over London in the next hour. I am sorry to tell you, but you will all lose your lives. I have taken your souls so that you will not feel pain or suffer. You will stay with me for at least the next few days... maybe even longer. It depends on how long it takes for people to find your body..." He trailed off.

Boone had often felt like he lacked the emotion he once had in his early years. But things like this still make his heart ache.

"We need to leave the city." He said, like they had a choice.

Chapter Fifteen

The hike out of the city centre was easy. They headed mostly west at a slight northerly angle. It was still another hour until the bomb dropped from when they left and the city streets had barely any people in them, let alone vehicles. Boone walked as he normally would, taking the footpaths, around streets, down alleyways and through gardens. The souls that followed still acted as their own intuition told them throughout their whole lives. So they dodged cars and tried not to run into each other. Realistically, if they had wanted to, they could have made it out of the city in significantly less time than Boone. Of course, it has to be mentioned that they, as souls, were no longer in danger of anything bad happening to them.

Once Boone and the souls were mostly out of the city, they headed for Marylebone. Berkeley Court, to be exact. The time was

4:05pm when they reached there. Boone ran the last couple of blocks just to try to make up as much time as he could. He ran into the building, completely ignoring the front door man and skipped up to flat 23.

Boone pounded on the door with his fist without stopping. Within twenty seconds, Maggie answered, looking scared at the sudden aggressive noise.

"Sorry, Maggie, the city is about to be bombed. You and I need to get out of here fast." Boone said to her as calmly as possible.

She didn't argue. She grabbed the keys to her and Dunlop's vehicle and raced down to street level. Leaving the building with Maggie ahead, they ran past the doorman, who had a rotary phone in his hand, talking. Boone only caught a few words as he passed.

"Beau Wainwright is here..."

It didn't matter. By the time Boone had hopped into the driver's seat of the vehicle and driven away, they would have been long gone. For now, they now headed completely north.

Part of the conversation that Boone had with Mary-Ann was the plan for after the souls were collected. He gave her a limit of 3:00 pm to collect as many as she could. Boone still wasn't sure how her Keeps worked, so wasn't sure what would happen if she missed some. Something unfortunately, that would definitely happen. Boone had told her to get to Wrotham Park by no later than 4:30 pm, which is when the first bomb would drop.

The drive was mostly quiet as Boone silently grew more concerned about Mary-Ann as time counted down. After ten minutes, Maggie spoke up to say she forgot to grab her handbag.

Then, every minute after that, she brought up another concern about her forgetting one thing or another.

"Maggie, you just need to be safe yourself. If your home gets hit, anything can be replaced very easily, you know that", Boone said to her.

They were almost at Wrotham Park with only a few minutes to go. Boone looked behind him to see the souls were flailing around as one mess of thin white cloud, almost like a flag flying behind the vehicle.

They reached Wrotham Park and Boone immediately hopped out and looked around for Mary-Ann.

"I'm here", she said as she stepped out from behind a tree.

Boone let out a visible breath, his shoulders dropped and his heart felt like it could beat again. Behind her were seventeen souls, who trailed her as they looked around confused.

Mary-Ann stepped towards Boone and stopped within a metre. She had a closed-mouth smile on her face, but tears in her eyes almost like she was trying to be brave in that moment.

He stepped forward and encompassed her in a hug. She broke down completely; a flurry of sobs came from her as her head rested under Boone's chin.

"You remind me of my daughter", he said.

She sobbed and sniffed. "You have a daughter?" She asked between crying. "You don't look old enough to have a daughter my age."

Boone lightly laughed at this. "You have a lot to learn." His laugh slowly faded as memories snuck back in. "I did have a daughter."

Boone, Maggie and Mary-Ann watched as hundreds of planes flew over the city in the distance, dropping bomb after bomb on the people and buildings below. The sound of dull thuds and sharp cracks came with light distant tremors, which permeated the ground beneath them.

Maggie and Mary-Ann stood with their mouths agape, watching it unfold. Boone looked with sorrow as he knew a new war had begun and this was just the start of it.

The following days were them all hunkering down in a small cottage style home just off the main road heading down to London. Boone had paid a recently widowed woman to rent her home for the unforeseen future only ten minutes down the road from where they met on the night of the 7th.

The bombings hadn't stopped and they all discussed whether or not it would be smarter to head up north more. Unfortunately, Boone knew this would be impossible as he or Mary-Ann would soon be called back towards the city for more souls. If Mary-Ann were more experienced in the matter, chances are she would be able to tell them all exactly when that was.

The next day, Boone sensed the oncoming vibrations of more souls needing to be lifted. Out of the fifty-four that he currently had tethered to him, forty-nine of them still remained. Out of the seventeen that Mary-Ann had, sixteen still remained. This meant those who were gone, were now in their final resting place. She still couldn't see them and most likely wouldn't for a while yet until her senses had become better. That would happen with time and meditation. For now, Boone helped her souls to understand what had happened and what would happen next.

Mary-Ann and Boone took Maggie's car close to the city, but not so close that they could see the destruction yet. They climbed out of the vehicle and walked the rest of the way. They couldn't risk the car being damaged and not being able to get out of the city, so this was their only option.

Once in the city, they split up, made their way to the souls they needed to collect and reconvened hours later back at the car. This back and forth happened every day for the next couple of months. Almost like a day job, they would pack a lunch each, hop in the vehicle and head for the city.

Every day that Boone went into the city, his heart broke apart more and more. He loved London, even though part of it didn't love him back. He was used to seeing the tall buildings and the beautiful gardens on his normal walks around London collecting souls. He got used to the lush green manicured front gardens and the expertly designed architecture as part of his life. Now, it was in ruins. The buildings were nothing but rubble. The fires that rang all over the city roared and smouldered until only dust and bricks remained of people's homes. The constant ringing of bells on top of fire engines could be heard every few minutes as the firefighters, risking their lives went from one fire or building to the next.

On the 21st of December, Boone was woken up once again to a rumbling through his entire body, like a truck was driving right through the cottage. He opened his eyes and stared at the ceiling while he mentally counted down the soul deaths for the day. He frowned and sat up from his cot.

"Mary-Ann?" he yelled from one room to the next.

Silence fell for a few beats before an unintelligible mumble returned as an answer.

"Are you able to tell me yet how many soul deaths you can detect?" Boone asked, now starting to stand up and putting on his slacks.

"Hmm? Oh, uh, I dunno", she said, clearly still have asleep.

Boone now stood at the doorway of Maggie and Mary-Ann's room. "Mary-Ann?"

She finally turned to this with her eyes barely open as she looked at Boone. She sat up and opened her eyes wider, seeing Boone's serious look on his face.

"I'm not sure still, I can tell it's at least ten... I think", she said.

Boone frowned again and left out the front door of the cottage without saying another word. The outside was cold but dry. The skies were completely blue from horizon to horizon. Mary-Ann, rubbing her eyes still, came out and hung in the doorway watching Boone, now sitting on the green grass outside with his legs crossed.

"Why the urgent wake up?" She asked.

"I only have one soul and I don't know why", Boone replied.

"Isn't that good?" She asked with a confused look on her face.

Boone didn't answer her. He still sat on the green dewy grass, legs crossed and now with his eyes closed. Boone drifted away into the void and then looked into the future. His eyes flashed.

He opened his eyes to Mary-Ann, standing right in front of him now.

"I'm in foresight", he said. "I'm going to go into the city and see what is about to happen and I hope I'm not dying today."

Boone quickly stood up and grabbed the keys from the table inside the cottage and hopped into the car, speeding off down the road.

He didn't do what they had been doing for the last few months and stop the car before the city. This was, after all, just a premonition of what was about to happen. He felt the pull of a lot of the souls dying today, but not his. He also couldn't find the glow as he normally would. This would be the first time in his life he wasn't able to locate one of the souls that were about to die.

Boone spent the next couple of hours trying to concentrate and look harder but still couldn't find anything. He drove along the outer perimeter of the city in an attempt to detect something, but nothing would come up. Shaking his head, he closed off his mind again, entered the void and came back out the other side. He was back, sitting on the grass outside the cottage.

"Boone?" Mary-Ann asked.

"Just went into the city, I couldn't detect anything. I need to concentrate and stop detecting the other souls in the city that are dying. I don't normally have this much competition, so it never gets in the way", Boone replied.

Boone once again closed off his senses to the world but did not travel into foresight or view into the future. He sat on the grass, trying to close absolutely everything off around him.

After centuries of experience, closing off the outside world was easy. He shut his eyes and they drained from a darkness with light blotches to nothingness. He then closed off his hearing as the birds in the trees and the slight breeze from the wind got less and less, eventually to nothing. The smell of the green fresh earth below him was mostly physical as he shut that off by stopping his breathing temporarily. Second to last was the feeling of the dewy grass tickling his ankles and wet pants from the moist ground.

The last was the hardest. He needed to completely switch off his brain so much that one by one, each soul that was weaker than the next would stop pulling him in, one way or another. He concentrated hard and then softly as he closed off memory and thought, feelings and fear, then... nothing.

His eyes sprang open and he immediately stood up and looked behind him.

"It's not in London", He said. "It's in Liverpool."

Boone felt sheepish. With everything going on with the bombing of London, he'd completely forgotten that these things happened elsewhere. He'd spent the months going on the morning commute to the city, picking up the souls and coming back home and doing it all again the next day. But this time was different.

Boone looked at his watch and saw that it was almost 8:30 am. He knew that the trains still operated between London and Liverpool, even during the bombings, but wasn't entirely sure how long it took. He immediately got up and went to grab the keys off the table in the cottage.

"Lets go; you're dropping me off at the station before you head in." Boone said to Mary-Ann.

Before he knew it, Boone was on the train heading north towards Liverpool. The office ticket lady mentioned the ride took around nine hours, depending on whether the lines hadn't been bombed at any point along the way. This meant Boone would arrive in Liverpool at around nine that night.

Chapter Sixteen

The journey to Liverpool was uneventful, which in the context of war, was a good thing. A fear still struck every passenger as the train made its journey through the rolling hills and pastures of rural England during the daylight. That fear became more and more apparent as the sun slowly set and each passenger clung to their bags or their loved ones, ready at any moment to run from the train, avoiding the fast-moving bombs.

In most cases, the train arriving into Liverpool would slowly pull into a beautiful arched Victorian-style terminal where people would disembark onto the station platforms alongside thousands of other people and workers. On this particular day, the train slowly stopped near the station in an open field. Only a couple of hundred metres ahead of them stood the scarred remnants of the beautiful station, now charred and damaged. It was covered in sandbags with boarded-up windows and blackout curtains. The glass roof was completely open, having been damaged by the bombs falling nearby.

Just as the destruction of London tore a hole in the hearts of its residents, the same happened here in Liverpool. The ruins now stood where homes and shops once were. The smoke and fires still raged on as firefighters and locals attempted to put out blazes one after the other, as bodies lined the streets from whole families who had died. It was evident that the German warplanes had targeted this city just as much as London.

Boone couldn't help but feel for the devastation of the residents. More lives lost, more souls that weren't tethered or saved. Now they wandered the earth not knowing that they were in some type of purgatory, which even Boone didn't know how to get to or even help with. He knew that there was a Soul Keeper in the city as he could feel it but knew also that one person alone could not help everyone.

He needed to work out exactly where he was going before it was too late. The city was dark now and the German planes made a habit of dropping their bombs when people would be in their homes late at night. Boone closed his eyes and entered the void and into foresight. A flash of light in his eyes crossed over.

Boone entered the foresight. He almost slapped his knee, feeling like it was so obvious now that the soul was here and not in London. Repetition had made him so intent on getting down to the city every day; he had lost focus and couldn't work out why he couldn't find the soul initially. He looked across the town and spotted a singular obvious glow coming from fairly close to the river's edge. He set out walking toward the glow, feeling the pull as it tugged him along like a dog pulling a leash.

Barely three minutes into the walk, he heard the disturbing rumble of planes in the distance. Boone had hoped that the death of his soul would be because of a simple heart attack or perhaps a car accident. Of course, he knew that the chances of it being part of the actual war or bombings were more than likely.

What felt like only thirty seconds from hearing the engines of the planes, the first sound of bombs hit the ground. They broke between the silence of nothingness and the screams of people crying from within the concrete ruins. Like a giant walking across the city, the boom, boom, boom sent shivers down Boone's spine. He picked up speed to a run, just trying to get to the soul before his pathway was blocked.

He felt like he was racing the planes and badly losing. Running for as long as he could, he eventually slowed to a jog, then a walk, before picking up pace again.

"Why do these foresights have to be so real?" he questioned the universe while puffing, struggling to catch his breath.

The familiar pull of the soon to be passed soul kept tugging. From the internal grip on his stomach, he knew he was roughly halfway to where he needed to be. As though the universe wanted to curse him even more, the worst happened. He had just finished running, slowing to a jog and then stopping fully. Putting his head down and hands on his knees, he sucked in as much oxygen as he could trying to catch his breath. He heard the familiar sound of a slow whistle, which was getting louder and louder above him. He held his breath and looked up.

"Not again…"

He quickly snapped himself out of the foresight, bringing back his senses and vision into the real world. He looked up and observed the sky above. They were clear for now but he knew that within minutes he would hear the rumblings of the planes again. The one thing he did know was that he could get as far as halfway between here and the soul. It was without too much of an issue getting around people, over ruins and all the way without the chance of a bomb landing on him.

That's just what he did. He once again picked up speed and ran for it. This time it felt easier for some reason. Like the adrenaline running through his veins was working at double speed, knowing that his own life now actually depended on it.

He made it almost halfway a full five minutes before he did in the foresight. With this, he knew that there wouldn't be a bomb dropping on him right there and then, so carried on. The sounds of the other bombs around the city still echoed through his ears and each and every bomb that came from the planes was like a repeating record. The rumble of the plane, the whistle of it falling to earth, the colossal explosion and then last, the screams.

Boone was still twenty minutes away by running, but could see exactly where he needed to go. If he looked beyond the crumbled buildings that fell onto the street, he could look all the way to the end and see a rippled humming coursing through the air. In the distance, it acted almost like a beacon trailing to the clouds. Boone noticed he was running north, up Derby Street, which felt like a main road for the city. He took as much internal notes as he could about his surroundings, considering his life may depend on it.

Now that he knew exactly where he needed to go, he picked up speed and ran as fast as he could, almost like he had unlimited energy now. His heart raced, but knew that it would be over soon. A whistling sound came from above at that very moment.

"Crap! Not now!" He yelled into the street.

A mighty explosion rang out directly to the front right of Boone. The side of a flat crumbled instantly into the street throwing mortar and bricks directly at him. He dodged one brick, then two and three as they came flying towards him. The last brick, however, he didn't see. As he dodged the others and stood back up with a thankful thought, he turned back and saw a full brick flying directly towards his head. It hit him. He was knocked back hard; his body went limp and fell to the ground.

An unknown amount of time later, he regained consciousness, opened his eyes and looked up towards the dark sky. It was silent apart from the raging fires and crackling of buildings. He sat up and felt his head where a large gash now formed a prominent feature on his forehead. Bringing his hand down and looking at it, it was completely covered in blood.

That's not ideal. Boone thought as he stood up.

He was slightly dizzy and felt like he should just lie back down. He contemplated having a small rest and a sleep, just for a few minutes, before regrettably shaking his head to get that thought away. He looked down at his watch but saw nothing but smashed glass and a broken circular frame. The humming of a soul still alive stretched through the air, so Boone knew he hadn't been unconscious for too long.

He started walking again, this time taking it easier. It took him another fifteen minutes, but Boone reached Juniper Street and headed towards a building that was surrounded by a few firefighters. He stood out the front of the now ruined building, looking in. The roof had fallen and the walls had then collapsed after that, coming down with the weight of it all.

"Can I help?" Boone asked one of the firemen.

The fireman looked him up and down. "Normally with that cut on your head, I'd say no, but in this instance, we need all the help we can get."

Boone noticed that they were a team but were oblivious to the fact that there was someone still in the ruins. Boone picked up a bucket, making it seem like he was about to fill it with water from the truck. He walked towards the truck and then cut around to the other side of the building. It was difficult to see what was happening and even questioned the fact that whoever it was inside, was still alive.

He saw a small crawling space below two large beams, which used to be secured to the roof of the building. Boone lowered down onto his knees and pushed himself through the gap. He moved rubble and climbed over a section of brick wall to see an even deeper cavity going to the back of the house. Within a couple of minutes and moving precarious building parts, he saw a leg sticking out from a fallen section of the building.

He crawled to this spot and then around the other side of it. He couldn't stand up at all and it was becoming increasingly more obvious that even if Boone was a fireman, it would have been impossible to move anything without risk of other things falling. On the other side of the fallen brick wall, was a man. He was currently still breathing but knew that at any moment he would take his last breath.

"Hello", Boone said to the man.

He didn't really know what to say to him. He had helped millions of people pass through their lives, but it was rare to actually be the last person talking to them as they actually died. Boone reached out and touched him. A small amount of energy burst through Boone as he did. The man turned his head and looked at Boone, saying nothing.

"I'm here to help you in your last moments, I'm sorry to say", Boone waited for a reply, but nothing came.

The man lay still breathing in and out almost like normal. He wore a dark wool tunic with a helmet just off to the side of him, which was labelled 'AFS' for the auxiliary fire service. This man had risked his life to save Liverpool and the people and unfortunately now lay dying himself.

"I'm sorry", Boone said again. He wasn't sure why. "What's your name?"

"James", the man said with a breathy, raspy voice, slightly coughing after.

Boone nodded, grabbed James' hand and lay with him. He didn't leave this realm as fast as Boone expected, but that was okay. They held each other as James' breath got more and more shallow until he took his last breath and died.

Chapter Seventeen

The death of James felt like a heavy weight had been lifted off his shoulders. In one way, he knew he was taking the pain away from someone; at the same time, they were still dying. That feeling of ease was somewhat temporary as he once again started to think about his own mortality. Part of him was convinced that this soul, this moment in time, was actually the last. What followed on from this was mortal life. The other part of it was what was next on his journey. Maybe rather than the universe giving him death, it gave him a chance to help Mary-Ann in her own enlightenment. In either case, he didn't really know what to feel. He lay next to James' lifeless body, holding onto his hand for the next hour.

The journey back to London was uneventful. Of course, the same went on with catching the train back. The people grew concerned as the train left, became more relaxed during the journey and then once again fear snuck in as night fell and they pulled into London. It was frightening to everyone around. Their own demise hung solely on the sporadic dropping of bombs on the city, like they were playing Russian roulette with their lives.

Boone made it back to Mary-Ann and Maggie at ten that night, only one day after leaving them. They both looked more relaxed than Boone would have thought for them. He came through the door of the cottage and found them playing cards together on a small square table in the middle of the kitchen. They both got up at the very same time and hugged Boone for what felt like forever.

Boone gave a small chuckle. "I guess you're glad to see me alive still."

They talked for a while about the last twenty-four hours. Boone gave them the rundown of what had happened in Liverpool. Mary-Ann shared her own day with letting Boone know about the dozen souls she collected that very day.

"Oh!" Mary-Ann perked up partway through their conversation. "I can't feel any large hums, almost like I don't have any souls for the next few days at least! I mean... I still see the ripples people leave behind, but nothing big."

Boone left the comment linger in his mind. He had these 'ripples' that Mary-Ann described, but with the exception of a few over his life, he only saw the ripples upwards of twenty-four hours before their death. He didn't comment to Mary-Ann about this but wanted to remember it. This wasn't something that he could guide her through on his own. He knew that there was only one person in this world who could help. That person lived in Turkey.

"That's exciting. Almost like the universe has given you some time off work!" Boone joked.

"James?" Maggie interjected, asking about her husband, James Dunlop.

"He's fine", Boone said. "I can feel him. I just haven't gotten through to talk with him; his mind seems very pre-occupied, like he has a lot of souls to Keep."

Maggie nodded at this, a line of watery tears puddling in her eyes. Boone hugged her, assuring her he would be fine.

He turned to Mary-Ann. "You ready for an adventure?"

The very next day they were off. Boone left Maggie with a little money and instructions on how to get more if she needed it. He wasn't sure how long they would be, so told her exactly that. However, in the back of his mind, he didn't expect them back for at least six to twelve months, based on what they found when they got to Turkey.

They had a couple of bags packed and slung them over their shoulders as they began their journey. Their first plan was to get out of London and then out of England. They didn't plan any of the trip and because of the war, they couldn't have. They were going to rely on good old fashion bartering and begging.

They headed south, making a stop by the lake where Boone's money was, before doubling back and hopping on a train. A two-hour train ride put them in Southampton where they more than likely had an easier time getting out of London. Boone knew that although it's easier for him to get through the city now because of the war, they would still have his face on file and on signs in the airport. They needed a boat.

During the war, they had two actual choices of where to catch a boat from. Liverpool was one, but it was more military-focused and further away. So, they picked Southampton. It was used more for civilian vessels and Boone figured it would be easier, but not a guarantee.

Once they arrived in Southampton, they headed straight towards the port. They were lucky on their very first go. They met a man named Antonio who captained a merchant cargo vessel appropriately named 'Jeanne d'Arc'. With a bit of banter back and forth, Antonio agreed to let them passage between England and Gibraltar. Boone paid him two gold coins a head and also promised they would be deckhands over the next eight-day journey.

As they boarded the vessel, Boone nudged Mary-Ann and nodded his head at the name of the boat.

"Briefly met Jeanne in France as another Soul Keeper and I lifted souls in that region for a few weeks, travelling through."

Mary-Ann looked at Boone, an unsure expression plastered over her face. He couldn't tell what was going on in her mind. He thought it was either her thinking, 'This guy is cool, he knew Joan of Arc', or something like 'Okay, oldie', almost like it was her dad explaining all the old songs he loved. Boone chose to think it was the former.

The cruise from England to Gibraltar would normally have taken roughly five days to get there. However, because of the war, they would zip in and out of certain zones where Antonio had learnt over time where it was best to avoid because of planes flying above or other warships bearing down on him. They spent the days as deckhands, helping with cleaning or cooking, eventually acting as lookouts so others could sleep. During the night, they would completely turn off all lights or candles that they had burning, essentially making them invisible to anyone nearby.

On one of the nights, Boone and Mary-Ann sat on the upper deck of the boat, watching the waves as they gently bumped the side of the boat every few seconds. A thought had been plaguing Boone's mind for the last few days, but he was almost afraid to ask. He had never seen himself as invincible, far from it in fact. But he had somehow made it this far through life; he wondered if it would ever end.

Boone looked at Mary-Ann. "You mentioned ripples trailing behind people, all people, right?" he confirmed.

"Mhmm, I see ripples through everyone. Some bigger, some smaller... but... you do too, right?" Mary-Ann tilted her head and looked at Boone.

"No." He felt like this was all he wanted to say but knew that she would ask questions. He wanted to ask her one last thing before she realised why he was asking.

"Do you see ripples through me?"

Her eyes narrowed and brows squeezed tighter together. "Yes...", She said reluctantly.

"The reason we're making this journey is to get to someone I met a very, very long time ago. He was said to have been able to detect the death of everyone on Earth. He told me that as a child, he spent every day and night screaming at the noise to stop. The noise was the humming of death."

Mary-Ann looked down. She, too, had spent her younger life in misery with this curse that she had been given. Her parents didn't even stick around long enough to hear her first words. They couldn't deal with the constant terror that drove their minds insane. Sleepless nights that led to sleepless days ended with an abandonment of her as a baby.

"You just asked me if you will die one day, didn't you?" She asked.

Boone nodded. "I know I will one day. I don't want to know when it's coming up, but you will. You will carry this burden throughout your whole life."

The clarity of Mary-Ann's life crossed over the minds of both Mary-Ann and Boone. Of course, this clarity was a major revelation to her and what she had gone through in her life. The feeling of the deep humming was still painful to her, but with an answer to what it was, she felt relief, albeit small.

Gibraltar was both quiet and busy at the same time. The town felt like it was void of any emotion or real people and replaced with military and soldiers. It had been bombed in the last year by Germany, so most civilians had been evacuated to nearby countries. They wanted to spend as little time here as possible, so as soon as they were off Antonio's vessel, they headed straight for what they thought was the more civilian area amongst the naval ships.

Their next leg of the journey was to Egypt. This time, it wasn't as easy as just walking up to one of the captains and asking for passage. For starters, fewer people headed that way due to the treacherous crossing past Italy and second, no one trusted them.

That was normal at this point in time; you could only trust those you really knew. Boone at this current time, presented in his late thirties and Mary-Ann was actually twenty-one. To everyone they came in contact with, they were an unusual combo. Too close together in age to be father and daughter and too far apart for them to be automatically labelled as a couple. So, most people were on guard about spies from both the British and the German sides.

After going through what felt like every vessel and captain in the port, they decided they would call it a night and find somewhere to stay.

They didn't sleep in style that night. Their accommodation, although had an amazing view of the Alboran Sea, didn't scream luxury. They found a small outcrop of rocks that was far enough away from the buzz of the port, but close enough to see any new ships come in. They didn't think they'd sleep, but they both did within minutes of laying their heads down.

The day that followed was just the same. Even bumping up the amount of gold that Boone would offer didn't work; all that did was make them even more suspicious. It was the day before the new year of 1941, which meant that there were even fewer vessels leaving the port than they had hoped. Even during war, everyone wanted to celebrate and have a drink.

They couldn't afford to stay in Gibraltar too much longer. They had the money and they could afford accommodation if they really wanted it, but the risk of arrest was too high. The more that Boone and Mary-Ann asked around for transport, the more people became suspicious and almost instantly gave them a no before they even had the chance to ask.

With discussions regarding what they should do, they ended up crossing over into Spain. Mary-Ann was completely at Boone's will at this stage as she hadn't even left her country of birth, let alone London. Another country with another language and new customs was something she couldn't quite get fully confident in.

In Spain, they were able to catch a ride on the back of a trader's truck going north towards Alicante. Alicante was another port that Boone thought they might be able to leave from. He paid the driver one gold coin for both of them and were on their way.

They reached Alicante in just over eight hours. It was winter, so by the time they had arrived in the town and then eventually walked to the port, it was dark. They decided not to try their luck with the captains as soon as they got there. The idea of trying to win a ride over to Egypt at this time of the night may have just set off as many alarm bells as asking during the day in Gibraltar.

They were both exhausted at this stage. Sure, they had slept during the last night and the last eight days on the boat, but they weren't restful. They couldn't bring themselves to walk the streets anymore and needed food. They ended up finding a bar on the edge of the port named Juan's Tasca. It was dark when they went inside, but quiet. There was no music playing and most people inside seemed to completely ignore the fact that two seemingly outsiders who didn't look like they had their sea legs, just walked in.

It was somewhat eerie with people just staring into their mugs, not talking or singing. Almost the complete opposite of what you'd see at one of the pubs back in England. A thousand-yard stare played on the faces of half the people. Perhaps they had seen too much in these last couple of years, or even worse, lost too many good people.

Boone and Mary-Ann walked to the bar and took two seats facing the bartender.

"Dos cervezas, por favor", Boone said to the man, asking for two beers.

Mary-Ann was surprised when Boone carried on speaking Spanish to the man, asking him if he knew of anyone willing to transport two civilians to Egypt and secondly, if he knew any place they could stay for the night.

"You know Spanish?" Mary-Ann asked him.

Boone smiled into his beer. "When you're as old as I am, you pick up on a few languages here and there from around the world."

"So you've been here before? Where haven't you been?"

"I haven't been everywhere in the world." Boone laughed. "Borders of countries were... fuzzy. I might be able to tell you where I was in the world if there was a large mountain range or raging river, but what might have been in Columbia then, might not be now."

Mary-Ann nodded her head, trying to take that in. It was difficult for her as she'd never really travelled and had somewhat of a difficult life growing up, so learning about other countries just wasn't as important to her as learning how to read and write.

Boone carried on, "At one point in my life, I worked at a spice trader. I travelled between India and Indonesia, learning their languages, meeting their people, keeping souls. While in Indonesia, I met a man named Willem who captained a ship that was setting sail to find new trade routes. I joined his crew as I heard the humming death of one of his crewmen and I had a job to do."

At this point, Mary-Ann was listening to what Boone was saying, but she was stuffing her mouth with rice, beans and chicken, which the barkeeper had just laid down in front of her.

With a mouth full of food, she mumbled, "You had no choice?"

"No, I had to go. No choice... Anyway, we set sail and headed south down the coast of Indonesia. There were whispers from the locals about this new 'southern land' they would talk about. So we headed away from Indonesia and went further south until we did in fact reach land. It was a new island that no maps had ever had a record of. We knew we had just discovered something and it was big."

"We started to charter the land as we sailed. I drew the coastline as much as I could as we went. The captain pre-emptively named it 'New Holland'. We landed on a few of the beaches along the way until we actually discovered people living there. We traded with a few for fresh water, fruits and nuts before leaving again along the coast. One of the beaches we landed on was where some of the men died. I claimed their souls before they went onto the land and something happened. An impossible communication situation led to both sides being wary of each other and they fought."

"We drew a lot of the coastline before turning back towards Indonesia and heading home. It was an already established continent where the captain had planned on trying to bring trade to in the long run. Once we were back in Indonesia, I carried on with my own spice trade and the rest is history. That is what we now know as Australia. I've never been back but would love too someday."

Mary-Ann choked on the food she was still shovelling into her mouth.

"You discovered Australia! Holy crap... you are old."

The night progressed. With the help of the bartender and a small donation to him, they were able to find a single room within someone's home where they rested for the remainder of the night.

Chapter Eighteen

New Year's Day brought many more people to the ports. For what Boone and Mary-Ann thought might be another day that they had to stay in Alicante, their hopes sure had improved even just stepping out the front door.

They split up early in the morning so they could cover more ground. They thought it might look less suspicious if they both went solo for starters. Boone started towards the south of the port and walked north, whereas Mary-Ann headed south.

By mid-day, their luck still hadn't changed. Of all the ships and all the captains in port, everyone still thought of them as either spies or smugglers, not to be trusted. There were also the odd few who didn't even give them an answer and just laughed right in their face when they asked about going to Egypt. Apparently, it was also an impossible task these days.

"Let's get some lunch", Boone suggested.

They found a little shack that sold different meats and cheeses and sat down on some of the rocks once again facing the sea.

"We may have to walk", Boone said casually, taking a bite out of a whole tomato.

"Really? How long would that take?" Mary-Ann asked.

"A few months."

Mary-Ann looked at Boone, appalled that he would even bring that up. "A few months! A few months!" she repeated.

Boone looked smugly at Mary-Ann. It was the kind that you would normally give someone if you were telling them a crude joke. However, Boone was very serious about the fact that they might have to. He had prepared for the idea that this may have to happen, but didn't want to bring it up with Mary-Ann in case she outright refused to come.

"I don't know what you're playing at, mister!" Mary-Ann huffed.

Boone chuckled to himself and, without saying a word, watched Mary-Ann stand up and walk away. He watched as she climbed down the rocks gently towards the sand and just stood at the water's edge looking out.

They had only known each other for a few months now, but Boone felt he had bonded with Mary-Ann. She truly reminded him of his own daughter, who he loved and eventually lost. He knew that once they got to Turkey, there would have to be a big change for both of them, which meant letting go. But for now, they were together and Boone was happy with that.

Boone was lying down, looking up at the sky, partly daydreaming and partly planning out their trip, or at least as much as he thought would be the trip. He also didn't want to have to walk that long distance. Boone heard a mumbled voice talking and he sat up from his position and looked towards Mary-Ann.

Mary-Ann was standing side-by-side with a woman. Boone smiled at the sight and climbed down the rocks towards them both. The woman chatted away, pointing one way and then the next as they slightly laughed between the two of them.

She was taller than Mary-Ann, around six feet tall, with blonde hair and a peach colour to her skin. She wore a pure white dress, which went from her shoulders to her ankles and a white rose tucked behind her ear.

Just as Boone got close enough to Mary-Ann and the woman, they turned around and looked at him.

"Boone! This is Selene. She said that she might have a way for us to get out of Alicante." Mary-Ann said with such joy in her voice.

Boone smiled at Selene and walked over to her so he was only a foot away. She returned the smile back at Boone. They stood in complete silence, like they were communicating purely through eye contact.

"Hello, Selene."

"Boethius, it's been a long time. I trust you are well."

"I am always well, you know that."

She nodded slowly at Boone, closing her eyes as she did it, almost like she was entering her own mind to remember something.

Mary-Ann looked between Boone and Selene before she whispered into Boone's ear.

"Uh, how does she know you?"

Mary-Ann stepped back and turned back around towards Selene. She was gone. Her mouth fell agape at the seemingly impossible disappearance of someone.

"She was right...", Mary-Ann stopped mid-sentence as she turned around and watched Boone walk away, like a woman disappearing was a normal sight.

Mary-Ann threw her arms up in the air and yelled, "She didn't even tell us where to go for a way to leave!"

"Yes, she did." Boone yelled back, only just enough for her to hear.

Boone picked up his and Mary-Ann's gear from the rocks and handed it to her as she climbed back up towards him. Without saying a word, Boone started heading towards the port once more, Mary-Ann trailing behind him by ten paces, struggling to keep up. He stood at the highest peak and looked over the entire port and pointed towards a large wooden ship with a name painted on the side, which read 'Eurydice'.

"There she is!" Boone said excitedly.

"That? That looks like it's on its last legs and should have been sunk two hundred years ago."

Boone looked past the cracks, torn sails and tar. He traded that in for longing and fond memories. The Eurydice was beautiful. It looked old, sure, but the bones held it together strongly. It had long, flat teak planks that covered the entirety of the ship hull from front to back. There were multiple decks and masts, which were made of a mix of pine and fir. Empty portholes could be seen running back and forth down the sides of the ships from where cannons once stood. The three sails were completely red and made the ship look ten times more powerful than anything around it.

"Let's go!" Boone yelled and started running for the boat like a kid running home after school.

It was even more magnificent up close. Its scars repaired with black tar stood out like gold running through veins of stone. Boone swore he could almost smell the wood just from standing fifty metres from it. He couldn't stop smiling.

They walked towards a group of sailors who were loading all kinds of equipment on board. Everything from fruit and bread to gunpowder and art supplies. Mary-Ann gained more concerned as they got closer to the ship and noticed the large men who wore mean looks on their faces.

Boone walked up to the man who had a clipboard and was ordering around everyone else, shouting at them to grab this or take that. His voice boomed as he commanded his men like he was the general of an army, eyes frowned together like he was upset that every one of them was even walking near him.

"Reporting for duty!" Boone yelled, a smile on his face.

The man turned around towards Boone and his face weakened, his brows raised and his frown turned into a smile. A tough, rugged man had just melted and turned into a soft, tearful boy, almost like he had just locked eyes onto his own personal hero.

"Basileios! By the gods, it has been too long!" The man hung his head and put Boone's hand to his forehead.

"It's good to see you too, Lucius. I see you've been given control of Eurydice?" Boone said.

"Yes, Sir... When Omar Al-Bahari crossed over, he bestowed the ship to me." The man replied.

Boone turned to Mary-Ann. "Mary-Ann, this is Lucius."

Mary-Ann made a little curtsy to Lucius before turning to Boone and whispering, "How many names do you have?"

Boone smiled, "Lucius knows me best as Basileios, the same way you know me best as Boone. Lucius is a student of mine. He is a Soul Keeper, just like you."

Mary-Ann scrunched up her face. The cogs in her brain were constantly rotating when it came to trying to figure out Boone. How old he was, who he knew, how many languages he knew. From the outside, he looked like a regular guy, young, good looking and so... normal. The small peeks he showed were little exposures of personality that she wasn't sure if he would ever reveal if he didn't have to. She thought about his travels and still shook her head in the fact that he had discovered Australia. She couldn't help but think about what else was beneath that.

Boone and Mary-Ann wasted no time. They offered to help and ended up loading the cargo onto the ship alongside the other crew. The heavy boxes and large sacks of rice were just that to the casual observer. Of course, Soul Keepers didn't get paid for saving souls, so Boone was sure there was something else on board that many wouldn't know about.

They set sail only a couple of hours after loading up as the last load of gear and last checks to the ship were done. Boone took off his boots, stepped onto the deck with his bare feet and inhaled deeply. Almost like he was pulling up memories straight from the deck.

Lucius had done this trip between Spain and Egypt at least a dozen times since the war began. Each time he got more and more wise at the routes he took and what parts of the sea to avoid. A normal trip, which would have taken him just over a week, could now take up to three weeks because of the war. He and Boone sat down and discussed their travels and the need to get from Egypt to Turkey.

"There are a lot of dangers now Basileios, especially between Egypt and Turkey. There is fighting in the Mandate of Palestine, even with the British there."

Boone nodded. He was already aware after the Great War that there had been troubles brewing with the Balfour Declaration. Word or news always got to Boone one way or another, even if it took months just to get to him.

"I am aware, Lucius. I will be paying handsomely for safe travel."

Lucius sighed, "Basil, you don't understand. These people do not care about riches. They are in religious battles and they will kill anyone who gets in their way."

Lucious snapped his finger, "I have an idea! It'll only take us about twelve hours off course, but we can drop you in Kriti and you'll find an easy ride to Athens. You'll need to cross through northern Greece, but it's not far from Turkey."

"Probably safe", Boone said, tapping his fingers on the table. "Let's plan for that."

Boone wouldn't have normally given up his own original plans so easily if it weren't for the fact that he was aboard the Eurydice. He felt that whatever destination, whatever port at whatever time or date it was taking him to, he would be okay with that.

As the sun set that night over the water, it was calm and almost like the world wasn't in the middle of a war. Mary-Ann and Boone shared a room on the ship. They didn't mind and were now used to having next to no privacy away from each other. Mary-Ann didn't know it, but Boone liked the company. He liked the questions that Mary-Ann asked; it wasn't all about souls that they'd save along the way or what happens after death. But it was questions about the world, about people and why they did certain things or how we could help them. He could see that, at heart, Mary-Ann was still that girl going into the homeless camp to help the people who needed it most.

They woke the next morning to another calm, sunny day. Lucius wanted to skirt the African continent as much as he could to avoid any interception from either side of the war. So when Boone and Mary-Ann stood up on deck, they could see on the starboard side of the ship was the coastline of Algeria.

Chapter Nineteen

The Eurydice settled into a regular pattern of tracking along the coast of Algeria for the remainder of that day. The sea gave them easy flows and straight winds; there were barely any signs of other ships or planes overhead. This allowed the crew to ease their minds of concern, which was a rare thing. That second day ended and rolled into the third and then the fourth.

Libya was less than a day away and this is where the trouble might come in. It had been under Italian control for the last thirty-odd years and no one really knew what they would run into. Boone, Lucius and his second mate all huddled together over a map in the wheelhouse. Drawing invisible lines with their fingers as they traced routes, they discussed the possibility of enemy ships or clear passage. In the end, they all voted that still going along the coast of Libya would be safer, although not out of complete trouble.

Day five started with preparing to cross in front of Libya. The crew aboard the Eurydice were of all races and religions, so tension and concern rose for some, but not the others. There were a couple of Italians, as well as one German on board. Lucius could speak both German and Italian, but Boone was so fluent, even people from those countries couldn't tell that he wasn't from there. They decided to have the four of them leading each section of the ship, in case of interception from the enemy.

By ten that morning, they had crossed in front of Libya and it was an immediate change in scenery. The waters, although calm, were dotted with other ships on the horizon. It was assumed they were enemy ships, so the Eurydice made no sudden change in direction to not appear suspicious. In no less than thirty minutes, they had eight ships within sight. Tensions on the Eurydice started to grow and what used to be hardworking sailors turned into fidgeting children, constantly watching the sea.

Even Mary-Ann started to get worried at the sight of the enemy ships, which seemed to be growing in size, presumably getting closer. She hung around Boone like she was a lost cat following its mother about, just wanting to be held for protection.

"How are you not worried?" Mary-Ann asked Boone.

Boone looked at Lucius, who smiled back at him. "Tell me, do you see the coming ripples of death linger on the men around you?"

Boone put up his hand as Mary-Ann went to answer. "I meant more than normal, as in imminent death."

She shook her head. "But that doesn't mean that they won't try to capture us."

"We, as Soul Keepers, can see what may happen in the future; we have that ability. It is true that the future isn't fully written in stone, but deaths are. I know the future just by who will and won't die."

Boone sat Mary-Ann down on a half barrel. "Let me tell you this. What if we decided to attack one of those boats? We would have no chance of beating them. Chances are we would be defeated easily and fast. That tells me that we will in fact not attack them, they will not attack us. You and I will not die."

Mary-Ann mulled that thought over for a minute. Her face went from scrunched up, to her eyes wide open and then finally bobbing her head from side to side with acceptance. "Okay" was all she said.

An hour later, it was completely obvious that the enemy ships would be on them within thirty minutes. Boone was right however, he knew that no one from his team would die. But he could see a ripple coming from one of the ships that were coming for them. His destiny was set; he was about the Keep the soul of the enemy.

Boone was staring out at the ship that was coming straight for them. His heart rate rose slightly, as he knew this one would not be as easy as normal. Getting on an enemy ship in the middle of wartime was one challenge. Now, getting off without being suspected of murder, that was another challenge completely.

He looked towards Lucius who immediately saw the look on Boone's face and turned towards what Boone was looking at.

"Ah", he laughed a little. "Are you going to tell Mary-Ann?"

Boone sighed, "She'll know."

Lucius crooked his head sideways. "How? She's only new, right? How could she possibly see your Keeps this early?"

"I believe she is a Seer of Death."

Lucius immediately spun his head back towards Boone in shock. "What! That's not possible. You told me there are only ever three on earth at once."

"I know what I said." Boone was making a motion with his hands to get Lucius to quiet down.

He didn't want Mary-Ann to know anything about what he truly thought she was. It would all come out in time and hopefully through their contact in Turkey.

"For now, we just need to worry about that." Boone nodded his head towards the boat, which was fast approaching.

The enemy ship which they saw coming was accompanied by two other ships directly behind it. Boone, Lucius, the two Italians and one German were all positioned across the deck as the Italian vessel, now seen by its flag waving at the top, pulled up within fifty metres of the Eurydice, now stopped itself.

Across the deck of the Italian vessel were a dozen men, now pointing rifles at them. Within seconds, a loud crackling came over the speaker followed by an Italian accent speaking English.

"This is the Regia Marina! You are in restricted waters. Put down your guns and prepare to be boarded!"

Everyone on board the Eurydice looked around at each other. None of them were carrying weapons and as far as this enemy vessel knew, they didn't have any at all.

As though experts just going through a pattern, the Italian navy, Regia Marina, only took two minutes between calling out the boarding and actually stepping onto the deck of the Eurydice. The men who came on board wore typical white tunics and trousers, with flat sailor caps. They each carried rifles in their arms, which constantly pointed towards the Eurydice crew. The men were young, between eighteen and twenty-five years old. They bore nervous faces as though they were just following orders they did not want to carry out.

Following the white uniformed men was an older man, perhaps in his fifties. The man walked with purpose, as though he was someone who demanded recognition and respect just from the staunch looking face he presented. A dark blue uniform with an accompanying blue cap lay crisp across his body. A gold badge was firmly attached to the front of his cap. He did not carry a rifle but had a small pistol, which hung from his hip, ready to grab at a moment's notice. He was the captain.

The captain stood between his men and looked towards the Eurydice crew, trying to look intimidating, but came off to Boone as ridiculous. The man next to him spoke up in the Italian language.

"You have been stopped by the Maestrale vessel as part of the Regia Marina. We demand to see your papers!"

Lucius pulled out a folder, which contained fake papers, previously prepared by his team and handed them to the man without saying a word. He then handed them to the captain who spent the next few minutes reading them over carefully.

The Maestrale crew looked amongst themselves, almost like they were daring one of them to cause an issue, giving reason to open fire. Before that could happen, the captain put down the papers and looked towards both Lucius, Boone and then to Mary-Ann.

"You!" He pointed to her.

The blood drained from Mary-Ann's face, almost like she was seeing death in her eyes already.

"Uh uh, yes, uh, Sir", she said, as she struggled to find words.

"You are as white as the English; your red hair screams that of the enemy. Where is this vessel from!"

"Uh, um, we boarded in Alicante." Mary-Ann said.

Boone stepped forward and spoke to the captain in full accented Italian. "We boarded in Alicante, but we are a civilian vessel and not part of this war. We all hail from different corners of the globe."

The captain looked towards Boone, a twitching disgust crossing his face at the fact that someone had talked to him when he didn't question first. He glanced backwards at one of the soldiers, seemingly giving him some kind of secret signal. The soldier stepped forward and towards Boone. With his rifle in his hands, he brought it up and smashed it directly into Boone's nose, sending out a loud crack which echoed on the silent deck.

Boone didn't go down, but his hand immediately went up to his face, covering his nose and catching the mass amount of blood now trickling down his face.

Crap, that hurt. He thought to himself.

The broken nose that Boone had just sustained was nothing. It was painful, sure, but only temporary. He closed his eyes and focused hard. His nose started to move right on his face, moving back into place. He could hear the cartilage moving as it moved back into its original positioning and the bones re-setting around his cheeks. With his hands still covering his nose, he breathed in deeply through his nose to find it perfectly back to normal. He didn't wipe away the blood as that may have given away that he was fine and really didn't want another blow to the face.

The soldier who had hit him was now back in formation. Boone wasn't done yet. He knew that he would have to get onto the enemy ship, Maestrale, somehow and this may be the only way. The captain was still looking towards Boone, seeing if he made any more noise. Just as he turned his head back towards Mary-Ann, he did.

"We are not part of your war!" Boone yelled.

The soldier once again stepped out of formation with his rifle in his hands once again. This time, Boone fully expected it. The soldier brought up his weapon to Boone's head height within a split second, anchored back and swung it once more towards his face. This time, Boone grabbed the end of the rifle with one hand and flicked it away from his head. With that continued motion, he then spun the rifle completely around, knocking it out of the enemy hands and now grasped it with his own. He smiled at the soldier in front of him as his mouth fell open at the turn of events. Boone jammed the butt of the rifle back into the soldier's face, this time breaking his nose.

With what felt like less than a second, four other soldiers pounced Boone on, rocking him onto his stomach and handcuffing him as their knees dug into his back. They stood him up and marched him towards their vessel. Boone turned towards Mary-Ann who was now even more shocked at the turn of events. He winked at her, turned and was out of sight before anyone knew it.

The captain looked between the remaining crew on board the Eurydice. "Leave! Now!"

With this, Lucius waited for the enemy crew to cross back over onto their own ship. He raised the anchor, opened the sail and once again started to slowly drift away.

Mary-Ann rushed towards Lucius once she saw they would be out of sight and hearing distance of the Italian ship.

"We can't just leave him! Please Lucius!" She had tears in her eyes.

"Basileios is a god that walks amongst men; he is exactly where he needs to be."

Chapter Twenty

Silence fell upon the ship as it set sail once again along the coastline of Libya. The cracking of the wooden hull and the splashing of the waves were all that were heard as Mary-Ann stood in disbelief at what had just happened with Boone. She was now surrounded by people who might as well be strangers to her. Her emotions flowed in a repeating cycle of concern, worry, anger, acceptance and then back to concern.

She looked over the water back toward what she thought was England. Wishing as hard as she could, all she wanted to be was back in England. But she knew that there was nothing she could do could get her back there. She had to have faith in both Boone and Lucius.

⚘

Boone had just winked at Mary-Ann, trying to give her a signal that everything would be okay. He hoped that she wouldn't make any rash decisions like trying to leave the boat and instead, trust in Lucius as much as Boone did.

The crew of the Maestrale had dragged Boone across to their own vessel before throwing him down on the deck like he was just part of the cargo now. He went down hard. Without having his arms or hands to put out in front of him, he caught his chin on the decking and split it open. They picked him up again and dragged him once again. This time, down into the hull of the ship and into some kind of holding cell.

Two of the sailors threw him in there as another two watched. They spoke among themselves before locking the door, giving quick glances back towards Boone. If he could have heard what they were saying, he would have prepared himself more; unfortunately, he didn't.

All four sailors entered the cell, a look of disgust on their faces. Without a second thought, they started kicking Boone, one after the other, as he lay still on the floor. Their hard leather boots knocked the wind out of him and pummelled his body black and blue. They broke ribs, cut open his lip in two places and left one of his eyes almost hanging from its socket. As one last punishment and almost just to embarrass him, they stripped him of his warm clothing, leaving him with nothing.

He lay curled up nude in a ball for the next fifteen minutes just trying to ease any pain at all that he had felt. This time, with the extensive damage they had done to his body, it would have been impossible for him to heal himself and it not be noticeable. He breathed in and out slowly, struggling to catch his breath every time he tried to suck the oxygen in. He regretted the choice of getting onto the ship immensely.

The pain was even more unbearable once he stood up. He was sure that at least one bone in his legs was cracked and that there was an almost guaranteed break in his right arm. He looked up and around the room, seeing that he was now completely alone.

The room was clean, but completely metal and cold. The steel bars that hung from the ceiling to the floor looked completely polished, as though it was one of the sailors' jobs to clean them every day. The floor of the cell was clean almost to a polish. There was one bunk in the cell, which had a blanket on it, allowing Boone to at least sit down and wrap something around himself, trying to figure a way out of this predicament.

The empty, quiet and eerie feeling of the cell made memories flood back of his time in various prisons over his life. Boone wasn't a bad guy. In fact, everything he did, he did for the good of other people. However, being a Soul Keeper, just like in this instance, came with challenges that he needed to get over and get through. For now, he needed to wait and see what came next.

Hours passed and Boone still just sat in the same position on the bunk inside the cell, almost afraid to move for fear of something else breaking. Every minute felt like an hour and every hour felt like a day. As he counted in his head, the rhythmic waves splashing onto the hull of the boat gave him solace in everything still moving around him, showing that he wasn't alone.

As the sun began to set, he heard footsteps coming down the stairs into the cell room. Boone looked up and to the left and saw the very reason he had made the choice to get onto the vessel. The man who now stood in front of him, a tray of food in his hands, was dying.

The man didn't know this, of course, but Boone did. He could see the ripple course through his body and now that Boone was taking notice, he heard the humming of his death.

"Here, eat." was all the man said.

He held the tray in a small slot halfway down the cell door. Boone slowly rose from his seated position and with the blanket wrapped around his waist, walked over to the man.

Is this all that was needed? I had to come here just for this? Why did you send me for this soul?

Boone reached out slowly towards the man and held the tray. His finger brushed the side of the man's finger as the food crossed from one person to the other. A burst of energy rushed into Boone. He could feel it working through his body almost like a hot chocolate going down his throat.

"Grazie", Boone said to the man, as he walked back up the stairs and out of the cell room.

He turned around and walked towards the bunk and sat down once again. Looking at the tray, there were only a couple of mouthfuls of vegetable soup and one roll of bread. Boone wasn't that hungry but knew that this might be his last meal for a while, so ate.

"I'd share with you, but, know you. You're going to die soon anyway", Boone said.

He looked up to see the soul of the man he had just Kept. For only a split second, the man stood in complete shock, unaware of what was happening and why he was standing in the cell with Boone. Anger flashed into his eyes and he bounced towards Boone without a second thought.

Boone adjusted his focus and senses and phased the image of the man out of his sight. He wasn't going to put up with someone trying to attack him again, not now. Not that any soul could actually hurt anyone, he just didn't want to have to bother with the aggression.

Night fell upon the boat and Boone did his best to lie down and imagine the pain away from his body. He slipped in and out of sleep, almost like he was falling into comas every twenty minutes. At this very moment in time, he just wished for a soft mattress to sleep on, nothing else, just the mattress.

The night was tough, but Boone got through it. He was woken at seven in the morning by someone dropping half a roll of bread into his cell. It wasn't the same man this time, however.

"Where is the guy who gave me the food yesterday?" Boone asked, fully expecting no answer.

"Fell overboard. Gone."

Boone nodded and focused his senses again to see if the Soul was gone. He was.

For the most part, souls will find their final resting spot and move on to whatever may be next after their life on Earth. In this sailor's case, his final resting spot was the ocean. His body would never be found.

This day felt even more difficult. The pain in his body picked up immensely and the bruising showed all over his body. He imagined that if he could see himself in a mirror, all he would see would be a puffed out red, black and blue face.

The hours dragged as the only sound in the room was the banging of the waves on the side of the vessel. He counted them as they splashed, guessing based on the number of times he heard it as to what time of the day or what the weather might be like outside.

That day passed with no sighting of another person.

The next day was the same. The morning started off with pain and a want for a soft bed to lie on, but nothing more. Even the small bread roll he had the previous day was at least something that gave him time to pass. But no food or people came.

Two more days passed without so much as a sight or voice of another person. But that fourth day, he heard the steps again of another person walking down the stairs. He hopped up faster this time and waited at the door of his cell, trying to catch a glimpse of who it might be. As expected, it was one of the Maestrale crew members, but with a cup of water in his hand.

The crew member handed the cup to Boone, who took is gratefully and poured the water down his throat, thankful for even that small amount.

"Where are we?" Boone asked the soldier.

"Our captain has decided your fate. You will be dropped in Benghazi at one of the hospitals. From there, you find your own way."

The soldier walked away without saying another word.

Boone sat back down and took a deep breath. The last few days were bad, but could have been much worse. He knew once he was in the hospital, he could heal up fast and get out of there. He still wasn't sure where he was, but based on where they were when he got taken on board, he couldn't be more than a few days away.

The days went faster now as hope had taken over in Boone's mind. He didn't want that hope to be crushed too hard, so still took each day as it came, trying to count the waves on the side of the hull.

On the fourth day, he got his wish. The Maestrale pulled into the port of Benghazi, Libya. Boone could hear the mumbled yells of the people outside the ships trying to sell things to the vessels getting tethered to the port.

The footsteps of two people echoed down the stairs and walked to Boone's cell. Without saying a word, they opened the cell door and grabbed him by both arms and dragged him once again. The pain returned to his slowly repairing body as he felt the broken, unset bones in his arms digging into the nerves around them. Hot shock waves of pain travelled throughout his entire body.

They allowed him to walk up the stairs on his own and then onto the deck. Once the bridge walkway to the port was extended out, they brought him to the edge of the ship and threw him down the walkway. He stumbled as he struggled to catch himself from falling and causing even more injuries.

He looked back and the two who had thrown him had walked off without a second thought. He was free.

He turned around and walked towards the main city district. It was the first time he'd been in Benghazi, so wasn't entirely sure where to go, but that didn't bother Boone as there had always been a first for everything. The streets were busy, dusty and loud. The bruised look of Boone didn't deter anyone at all from trying to sell him their wares or some kind of vegetable or dead animal on a hook. He ignored them all as all he wanted at that time was a quiet place to focus.

Within twenty minutes of slow walking, the amount of people started to reduce as he left the main city district and wandered into a small village on the outskirts. He found the only tree he could find in the entire city and leaned against it, sliding his body down until he hit the ground. He grasped his arm, still in pain, just trying not to think about it.

He closed his eyes and focused hard. The noise around was almost completely gone, so closing off that sense was easy, as it was just the noise of the wind rustling the trees. His sight behind his eyelids turned from a red blood colour to complete darkness. The pain was the one he had the most trouble with. He breathed slowly, in and out, trying to increase blood flow through his own body just long enough for him to release the pain.

A flash of light passed over his eyes and he found himself in a completely colourless void of whiteness. His body felt the best it had in years he thought, as he stretched and jumped up and down, pretending to box and throw punches to an invisible enemy.

"Okay, while I'm here, let's go see some people."

Chapter Twenty one

Boone's eyes flashed once again, another even brighter white than he was already in and then went black. Time ticked down as he waited a few more seconds to bring his senses into focus. He opened his eyes to a cloud of dirt flicking up towards him. The sound of bullets whipped around his head as he instinctively ducked down to avoid any projectiles connecting with his non-physical self.

He looked to his left, down the path of a dirt trench and young men cowering down, hugging their rifles and themselves. The distant look on their faces told him exactly where he was. He looked to his right, directly into the smiling face of Dunlop.

"Hey Boone!" Dunlop said to Boone.

"You almost look happy to see me!" Boone yelled into the continuous noise of gunfire.

"It's good to see you, that's for sure! Is Mags okay?"

"Yes! The last time we saw her she was fine. I'm not sure about your flat, but she's safe."

Dunlop shrugged. "That's okay; she's all that matters! Who do you mean by 'we'?"

"New Soul Keeper, I think she's a seer! I'm in Benghazi, Libya. I got caught by the Italians and am trying to catch up with her now."

Dunlop nodded as he pulled his head down and shoulders up, shielding his neck from a nearby explosion. He didn't have a rifle in his hands like the rest. A bag with a medical cross on it hung across his shoulder, which told Boone all he needed to know about Dunlop's position in the army.

"A new seer is a big thing, Boone, are you sure?"

"There is doubt, but I'm heading to Turkey." Boone motioned to the bag Dunlop was holding. "You healing or just a medic?"

Dunlop twisted his flat hand back and forth to say, a bit of this, a bit of that.

"How many years have you lost?" Boone yelled over another volley of speeding bullets.

"Not that many", he said, slightly shrugging his shoulders. "Fifteen... sixteen, or so."

Boone could see that he had aged. The stress of what and what it looked like on Dunlop's face was something he knew well. It was something that he could never forget. New lines creased the sides of Dunlop's eyes as he talked. The bags under his eyes drooped and the look was the famous thousand-yard stare. He had been in the war for far longer than anyone else would have been. The consequences that Dunlop could face if he were here for another twelve months could mean him returning to London as a fragile old man.

They both smiled at each other one last time. "I have to go", Boone said.

A silence lingered between them both for a few seconds. "Look after her, Boone."

Boone nodded once more and phased out of existence in Dunlop's view. Boone's eyes flashed a white bright light again before he was dropped onto the deck of the sailing Eurydice. He stood behind Lucius and Mary-Ann as they both looked out on the water, observing something in the far distance.

"Hope you're not having too much fun", Boone said.

Lucius spun around and saw Boone; he instantly had an enormous smile on his face.

"Basileios! By god! At least you are alive, my master. Tell us where you are!"

Mary-Ann spun around after Lucius's excited tone. She had a smile on her face as she turned, but it slowly faded with the realisation that Boone was not actually there.

"Lucius? Who are you talking to?"

Both Boone and Lucius looked at each other and perhaps Boone just a slightly more guilty. Mary-Ann had been in training for the last year, but the training wasn't as normal as Boone would have liked. They weren't able to sit down and talk about focus and senses, not aging or healing or anything like that. They had focused purely on Keeping the souls that the bombings of

London had thrown at them. Boone felt guilty because Mary-Ann did not know even some fundamentals of being a Soul Keeper.

Boone laughed, "Can you just give her a quick rundown. She only doesn't know how to see me because I've never told her this was possible. She doesn't need some magic power, just needs to know it's possible for Soul Keepers to cross realms."

Lucius shook his head. "Okay, Red, listen up. Basileios is here. As a Soul Keeper he can cross over realms to those who he has a special connection. They need to be kind of thinking about him at the same time. Just close your eyes and believe it and it'll work."

Mary-Ann did just that. She closed her eyes for ten seconds and mouthed to herself that she could see Boone; in fact, she begged to see him. Ten seconds later, she opened her eyes and there he was, standing right in front of her only a few metres away.

She ran at him with her arms opened, but before he could say anything, she phased completely through his body and out the other side.

"What on earth! What happened!"

"I'm not really here, Mary-Ann, I'm in Africa at the moment. This is something we as Soul Keepers can do." Boone shook his head. "I'm sorry. I've made you under-prepared in your life. Once we meet up, we'll run through some things. In the meantime, Lucius will still drop you in Kriti. I will meet you there in one week and we will head to Greece."

Boone looked at his wrist where his watch used to be, sighed and then looked at the sun in the sky.

"I need to go. I need to talk my way onto a ship from here and hope someone is going to Kriti. I'll see you soon. Mary-Ann... I'll be here. I can hear you if you really need help."

He vanished from Mary-Ann and Lucius's sight and within a second, reappeared in the white endless void once more. He didn't need to focus very hard to get back to his actual body; that was as easy as waking from a dream you knew wasn't real. The hesitation was the healing of his body. He was pretty sure he'd be healed by now but wasn't sure if he should have gone back to Maggie Dunlop and given her some sort of sign from beyond the realm.

In the end, he decided it would be best to head back to his body and see if he could get an actual letter to Maggie to let her know he was fine.

As though waking from a dream, Boone opened his eyes and stared at his surroundings. As expected, he was where he had been only minutes earlier, still leaning against the tree. He looked around to see if anyone nearby would have seen a miracle happening right in front of them but couldn't see anyone. Examining his own body, he knew straight away from the lack of pain and being able to move quickly that he was mostly healed up. He lifted his arms, inspecting them like he was picking out a piece of fresh fruit at the grocer's. He then patted down his legs, waiting for the bruised pain to come screaming through again, but felt nothing.

With feeling like a million bucks, he stood up and his body cracking sent a shiver through his spine like he'd been in a month-long coma.

Okay, maybe not a million, he thought to himself.

The next item on his agenda was getting back to Mary-Ann, who should be close to getting to Kriti. He needed transport in a strange land, with no money and no contacts. The first thought was heading back to the port of Benghazi; however that could lead to a bad idea if the Maestrale crew happened to see him.

Boone walked to the shops once again, heading towards the port but still staying far enough away to not get caught. He looked at the shops that he was passing, which were mostly food and a few selling clothing. Nothing that could immediately help him.

That afternoon was spent scouting the area and mentally writing off certain places, people or groups as being a possible escape. The sun was setting in the sky and the people in the streets were all packing up and heading home. Boone was about to give up for that day and he saw what he could only describe as a shining beacon of hope.

His eyebrows went down, almost like he was angry at himself for even thinking what he saw was actually real or plausible. Nevertheless, he picked up the pace and jogged to what he saw. Thirty seconds later, he stood looking into a shop window, mouth agape. The shop was called S. Adam's - Men's Apparel.

Shaking his head out of a daydream, he quickly reached out for the door of the shop and walked in. His head spun around trying to locate the same man who had helped him in London.

"May I help you, sir?" A voice came from behind him, speaking perfect Arabic.

He spun around and looked in the direction of the voice. He was a dark-skinned man, perhaps in his mid twenties. He wore a perfectly fitting blue and red checker patterned suit with a black bow tie around his neck.

Boone didn't know what to say. In his mind, he expected to find the same man as was back in London, almost like he was some kind of magician, travelling between counties just for Boone's own personal service.

"I need transport", Boone said to the man.

The man looked at Boone like he was crazy. Which, on all accounts he may very well have been at that point.

"I'm sorry, Sir. We make tailor made formal wear..." Silence fell between them both. "My name is Horo." He reached out to shake Boone's hand.

Boone lingered, looking down at Horo's hand and then back at his eyes. He wondered if this was some kind of trick, some kind of illusion playing with his mind. He brought up his hand and accepted the handshake.

"Boone", he said, not adding anything extra to it.

"Well... Mr Boone, I'm not sure you are in the correct location. As I stated, we tailor formal wear and sell it all over Africa."

Horo looked down at Boone, taking in his dishevelled appearance. Boone was covered in blood from his time on the Maestrale. No cuts or bruises to prove where it came from, just blood. He still kept his shoes, but even those were half untied, making him almost like a lost toddler waddling into a random shop.

Horo opened his mouth again to talk, paused and then changed what he was going to say. "I'm just about to sit down to a meal; how about you join me?"

Boone shook his head slightly from side to side, trying to snap himself out of the delusion of this not being true.

"Sorry, Horo. I understand how I look, but I need passage." Boone said.

Horo looked at him quizzically, but did not immediately correct him, saying he was in the wrong place.

Boone looked around the shop, finally taking it all in and trying to work out if this indeed was somewhere that could help him. His eyes wandered along the long racks of jackets, pants and shirts, up to the hats and along to a shelf of ties and paused.

He walked over to the rack of ties, which sat perfectly along six wooden boards behind them, perfectly blending in with the remainder of the shop. He walked to the window, looking out to see if there was an empty space behind it. There wasn't. In fact, there seemed to be a randomly placed, nondescript building right next to them with a single door being the only way in. Boone looked up and noticed it also didn't have any signs to show it was a retail outlet.

He walked back to the rack, eyeing every tie, every hook and crack in the wood. He smiled a little and turned back towards Horo and pointed to the tie rack.

"I need passage", Boone said, now with a little smile curling up at the corner of his mouth.

Horo's eyes snapped wide in concern. "Who are you?" His voice slightly lost confidence.

"Please contact Mr Adam and let him know Boone is here and needs passage to Kriti."

Chapter Twenty Two

Within twenty-four hours, Boone was on a shipping vessel off the port of Benghazi, heading straight for Kriti. The vessel, which was sailing had full access and papers to show, should any Italian ships stop them in the water, not to mention they were flying the Italian flag. Because they were sailing direct and hopefully without the interference of enemies, Boone estimated he would arrive in Kriti roughly the same time as Lucius and Mary-Ann. If not, it wouldn't be long after that.

Boone was a lot more relaxed on this part of the journey than he had been since they arrived in Spain. They knew where they were going; they knew how long it would take and they knew they had free passage.

"Would you like some lunch, sir?" Horo said in a perfect English formal accent.

Somehow, Horo had been given orders to stick with Boone through whatever journey he needed or until Boone said otherwise. As soon as Boone heard this, he immediately told Horo he didn't need him. However, still ended up with him on the ship, going to Kriti.

Boone and Horo spent that first day learning everything he could about Horo and how he ended up working for Stuart.

Horo was born in 1920 in Ethiopia to a farming family. They were poor, but gave Horo everything they possibly could. He was raised speaking Arabic, with his parents teaching him as many words as they could in English. He never went to school, never had any education as a child and worked day in and day out from when he first started walking, just to help out his family so they could all be fed.

When Horo turned sixteen in 1935, there was an invasion of Ethiopia by the Italians. Horo was taken from his family, given a simple spear and forced to fight during the war. He was lied to and manipulated into fighting with the threat of his family being killed. So that's just what he did. He spent months with other teenagers who each had their own weapons, from old World War rifles and grenades to simple spears like Horo. They ended up killing a few people, but the Italian forces were just too much for them and killed almost everyone in his group. Horo sustained major injuries to his upper body, with five gunshot wounds and a large gash along the front of his body from shrapnel.

In 1936, when he returned home to heal, he found his parents dead in their home, seemingly having been targeted alongside a neighbouring village by the Italian invasion. Horo didn't spend any longer than he had to in that home. He picked up his meager belongings and made his difficult escape out of the country, eventually ending up in England, seeking asylum.

During his first year in England, a family of which Stuart was the head took him in. Stuart sent him to school, homed him and fed him like he was his own son. He taught him everything he knew about sewing, fabrics, design and tailoring. He had him work in the shop in London for the next few years after that.

Horo found his way back to Africa during a large shipment that S. Adams was sending over to Egypt. They stopped in Benghazi to replenish their food and during that very small window; he met a girl who he would fall in love with. With the help of Stuart, Horo was able to establish his own shop in the main city of Benghazi. He sold to the locals and the Italian military, gaining information from them as he did and sending that information back to England. The rest is history.

The next thirty hours on the vessel flew by as though they were on a casual cruise around the world. No other ships stopped them, came near them or even took a second look at them. They were, in the eyes of the Italians, invisible. Horo would continue to talk with Boone about his life, growing up in Ethiopia, the war and moving to England. He was so thankful for the life he currently had and the girl he said he wanted to marry, who turned out to be named Zahra.

As they pulled into port in Kriti, Horo offered to see him across to mainland Greece to ensure a safer passage, but Boone declined. They'd enjoyed their short time together as they spent most of it talking and Boone trying to teach Horo how to play chess to mostly a failed attempt.

As Boone walked off the trade ship, he looked around to see if he could see any sign of the Eurydice along the port, but nothing stood out. He continued to walk along the beach with the idea of trying to find somewhere to eat, then realised he still had no money. He knew that once he got back to mainland Greece, he could track down a hidden cache of old Drachma.

He sat down on the beach, almost in a huff as he hit the sand. He watched over the ocean, thinking back on the last couple of years of torture, pain and Soul Keeping. He felt like he'd barely had even a second to think during this whole time. The only time he had enjoyed of late, was when he was travelling with Mary-Ann, who he now considered more and more like a long-lost daughter.

As though he was almost calling for her, he glanced over the ocean and saw the undeniable sight of the Eurydice cutting across the horizon, aiming for the small port of Kriti. He pounced up and started running for the port, thankful for his recovered legs.

He waited patiently for the next thirty minutes while the Eurydice slowed, bit by bit just waiting to enter the port and get tied up. Boone could see Mary-Ann standing on the bow of the ship, her hands above her eyes to shield them from the sun, looking towards the port looking for him. He smiled and raised his hands way above his head to say, 'I'm over here!'.

Mary-Ann spotted him and he heard the scream travel across the water as she jumped up and down constantly like an excited fan.

The Eurydice pulled up alongside a dock and before it even had a chance to get tethered down or a walking bridge across, Mary-Ann threw over a net and started to climb down the side of the ship. She ran towards Boone as he opened his arms and engulfed her entirely.

"I thought I'd never see you again! I can't believe you're okay." She backed up and looked over him from a distance. "They didn't hurt you or anything!"

Mary-Ann examined Boone as she trailed up and down his body, picking up his arm and looking it over to make sure he was okay. It took Boone back to when he first saw Mary-Ann, helping the tramps and homeless at the camp, getting them blankets and medicine when they needed it.

As soon as she saw he was okay, she looked him dead in the eyes, her face formed into an angry, sullen look. She punched him on the shoulder.

"Don't you ever do that to me again!"

Boone slowly rubbed his shoulder and smiled at her, pulling her to him again and hugging her.

The reunion with Lucius and the Eurydice went much the same way, minus the exclamation about the Italians hurting Boone. Lucius has assumed they did and he had healed up at some stage. They'd both been through it before and he knew just as well as any other older Soul Keeper that it's the same no matter the place or time.

Lucius and the Eurydice's next leg was heading on from Kriti and heading towards Alexandria in Egypt. Before that happened, the crew all decided it would be best to have a sleep on land and stock up as much as they could before setting sail again the next day.

Lucius, Mary-Ann and Boone all sat down at a small shack just off the beach, which sold all sorts of meat and fish. They all sat in silence, thankful for the last two and a half week journey from Spain to be now over.

Lucius was the first to speak. "I have bad news for you, Boethius... I've heard that the Germans have taken over Greece and you may need special papers to cross borders."

Boone was sipping a cold pilsner as Lucius said it. He put it down and thought for a very long second.

"I've had to cross borders in much worse conditions. Perhaps I need to practice my German before we cross", Boone looked at Mary-Ann. "You, my dear, will have to keep quiet while we are over there. You will be my daughter until we cross into Turkey."

He knew what she was in for once they reached Turkey, so he didn't even bother trying to teach her any of the language.

"Another thing, you have some money stored over there I would imagine?" Lucius enquired.

"I do. Enough to last ten lifetimes over should we need it."

"I've heard that Hitler is flooding the economy with drachmas. Your savings may not even be enough to buy a loaf of bread."

Boone sat for a moment in silence thinking, "I guess I'll load up here and hope for the best. I believe I do have some gold I can trade if I need something urgently."

The sun set and they all went their separate ways. Lucius paid for his entire crew, plus Mary-Ann and Boone, to have a few rooms to sleep in at one of the inns in the small port town. Mary-Ann went to her room to sleep, while Boone chose to head down to the beach once more. He ended up falling asleep on the beach, watching the waves crash into shore.

Chapter Twenty Three

"Wake up, Las, we've got a ride!" Boone yelled through the closed door of Mary-Ann's room.

He heard the dropping of Mary-Ann's body as she fell out of bed trying to sprint for the door. The excitement of her realising that something had actually gone right for once was mind blowing to her. No more scouring the ports, no more begging captains and crews to work for their rides.

They spent no time at all packing up. They raced over to Lucius and said that goodbyes and hurried down and boarded the ship that had given them free passage from Kriti to Piraeus in Athens.

The trip was fast, almost faster than anything they had done so far. It turns out Boone had given them a promise of a deckhand, but the trip only lasted less than two days, so he ended up enjoying the time doing menial tasks. It was also doing shipments for the Germans, so they didn't have to worry about getting stopped or having to go through any checkpoints once they reached mainland Greece.

As soon as they were off the ship, they didn't want to hang around. One of the sailors on the ship gave them word of trains heading between Athens, across northern Greece and into Turkey and in particular, Istanbul. Boone and Mary-Ann made their way to central Athens and towards the station where they knew the trains would be departing from. It took them half the day, but they got their there in the end.

Once they reached the station, it was crawling with German soldiers at all entrances and on every platform. They could see that there were checkpoints where the soldiers would be checking papers or travel permits to ensure the people who were going in and out of the city and the country were who they said they were. Looking around the station, there were signs and posters that reeked of biased propaganda. It was like a completely different country and life than Boone had seen previously.

Boone and Mary-Ann watched from the doorway of a shop no less than two hundred metres from the main entrance to the station. They didn't have any papers or permits and Boone had not come close to getting near his cache, which may be useless anyway. They needed a way to get past the guards.

He told Mary-Ann to stay behind and just hide for now. He went out into the street and started to walk down, watching the people as they went in and out of the building. He looked around the station to see if there was any way that they could sneak into the station. Even if they did, the next trouble would be two people getting onto a train without a ticket.

Boone turned around and walked the other way past the station entry again. He continued to watch the people as they filed in one by one. He noticed a pattern that came out of confidence, or maybe rightly so. He quickly walked back to Mary-Ann grabbed her by the hand and hurried her down the street past the station.

They stopped three hundred metres away, crossed the road and started to walk back towards the station. Within two hundred metres, Boone quickly took a long black jacket off the chair of a man who had his back to the street eating a meal. Boone quickly put it on, did up the buttons and told Mary-Ann to walk close behind him with her head down.

They reached the gate and joined the line behind two other people. Boone stood up straight and stretched out his back, pointed out his chin and waited for their turn next.

"Papers", the German man said, either unimpressed or bored out of his mind.

Boone stood without saying a word. He stared down at the man sitting on the chair in front of him and two men with rifles to the side.

The German man gulped, "Uh, papers, sir."

Boone stared again, his upper lip curling at the man in a sign of disgust. Then, he spoke perfect German.

"Papers... Papers!" Boone slammed his fist down onto the table so hard that even the men with the rifles flinched. They looked at each other, not knowing what they should be doing. "You insult me in front of Friedrich Adler's daughter!"

Boone closed in on the man who was asking for the papers. With only five centimetres between each of their faces, the German man started to shake and stutter his speech.

"I'm sorry, sir, that won't happen again. Please carry on."

Boone straightened his back again without taking his eyes off the man. He walked around the table and away from the checkpoint, Mary-Ann following closely behind without saying a word.

They went around the corner and stopped next to the station platform.

Mary-Ann jumped around to the front of Boone and looked directly at him with her mouth fallen open with a half smile. "Good lord! How did you do that! I've never... Wow!"

Boone smiled at Mary-Ann, getting more towards his relaxed state. "Nothing to worry about, all under control." He winked at her.

"Who is Friedrich Adler?" Mary-Ann asked.

"Just some guy I used to fish with a few centuries ago."

"Of course", Mary-Ann rolled her eyes.

Boone and Mary-Ann boarded the train without any more issues from the German patrols. They weren't sure, but they had hoped that on the other side of this train journey there wouldn't be another patrol waiting for them, ready for an arrest. They didn't want that thought to plague their minds during the trip and decided they'd deal with that when the time came. Boone did have the thought of keeping the long black jacket, just in case. He could always pull out his inner angry German if he had to.

They crossed through Athens and up north, travelling through the more rural areas. The scenery went from buildings and ancient architecture to lush green grass and farm animals. They eventually reached Thessaloniki where they had to leave the train and get onto another one heading towards Edirne, then onto Turkey.

At none of these points were they given any sort of grief or stopped for any reason. They started to think maybe someone had sent word of someone important transporting the daughter of Friedrich Adler and not to mess with him. But they only laughed this away as being doubtful.

They eventually made it to Istanbul where they once again hopped off the train and luckily straight onto another a third train, which would take them to Ankara.

The ride to Ankara was a thirteen-hour journey, so they both settled into their seats for the long ride. Mary-Ann pulled out a book and started reading it, trying not to fall asleep as she went.

Roughly six hours into their journey, Boone heard the voice of a woman encouraging her son. He looked up to see that they were both looking towards Boone and Mary-Ann. Boone tilted his head sideways to look at the boy as he held a book out in front of him, walking directly towards them.

"Hi", the boy said nervously.

"Hello", Boone said, smiling at the boy. "I like your shoes."

The boy's eyes lit up and he smiled widely.

"Thank you, mister. You look like someone from my book!"

"Oh, is that right? What book is that?"

The boy held up the book, which read 'Biblical people through time'.

"You are Basileios of Antioch!" the boy yelled.

Mary-Ann made a small yelp from Boone's side.

"Well, wouldn't that be amazing if I really was." Boone smiled at the boy.

"That WOULD be amazing! He fought the demons and healed entire villages of people! They say he could fly too!"

"I'm very sorry." The boy's mother interrupted as she stood up from her seat. "He has a very vivid imagination."

"Of course, that is good for a boy his age."

The mother slowly dragged her son back to their own seat while he never took his eyes off Boone.

Boone gave him a wink and put his finger up to his mouth to say 'Shh, keep it our secret'.

Secrets, lies, hidden facts or just straight avoidance was the norm for Soul Keepers. Mary-Ann was slowly learning this over time with everything that she had not only seen from Boone, but now from Lucius too. The only difference was that while Lucius had told tales of Basileios, Boone had shown her firsthand. In her eyes, he acted too normal most of the time. To her, he acted his age.

She watched Boone as the boy asked him questions and showed him the book he was holding. She took in Boone and his expressions, his slight smile and kind eyes. For the first time, she really noticed something different... wrinkles.

"What is your real name?" Mary-Ann asked Boone.

Boone looked at her with a half smile. "Boethius is my real name..." A silence lingered between them. "You have questions. I know you do. Whatever you want to ask, I'm okay with answering. But I am also here to protect you."

Mary-Ann's eyes went down to the ground, almost like she was trying to think of the most important questions first, almost like she only had a limit before they ran out.

"Some people call you Mr Boone. I know that isn't your real name but that's the name you chose."

The question lingered in the air with Mary-Ann almost willing Boone to finish the question for her.

"I am known as Boone, but not always. As you know, Lucius calls me differently, the same as other students of mine have taken on different names for me in the times that I have been their master."

"Boone is not a last name. If you were to look at the ID I had in England, it would say 'Boone Stone'. I've been known by this name for the last ten years."

"I know you are old... very old. But I thought you didn't get older. You look more tired and exhausted than you did back home."

Boone knew this question was coming. He figured that Mary-Ann was just so happy to see him that she had overlooked the obvious.

"I am old, or at least I feel that way mentally. As Soul Keepers, we have to assume our human age. I assumed that when we first met, I was around thirty-eight, give or take a couple of years. Now, I am around forty-five."

Boone continued, "Before you ask how I aged seven years in only a couple of weeks, there is something you need to know about being a Soul Keeper."

This conversation has played out repeatedly in Boone's life. From master to student, from husband to wife and from father to child. He knew exactly what to say and how to say it. He knew the questions that would follow before he even had the first words come out of his mouth.

He told Mary-Ann everything to do with aging, energy, healing and life. He gave her the speech about responsibility and more importantly, death. Part of him wanted to give her every little detail that he could think of. However, he knew that her life was about to change again once they reached Göreme. He knew that her life was about to be led through secrecy and a long training process.

The rest of the journey was spent sitting and talking between the two of them. Mary-Ann, just like those before her, asked the same questions that Boone had grown accustomed to and Boone was more than happy to answer most of them.

They reached Ankara in what felt like record time before jumping onto their last train heading down towards Kayseri for the next leg of their journey.

Chapter Twenty Four

As much of a significant impact England has had on Boone's life, the same could be said about the Kayseri region. It was here that he met new people, learnt the way of the monks and discovered more of his inner self than anywhere else before that. More importantly, it was here that Boone met the seer known as Theron. Theron now resided in the neighbouring settlement Göreme.

As Boone and Mary-Ann stepped off the train into the busy Kayseri train terminal. It had been multiple lifetimes since Boone had been here. The grounds in which he stood barely looked like anything he had remembered from his past, so any reminiscing simply didn't happen.

"No train", the woman at the ticket office said to Boone.

They hoped that the last leg of the journey to Göreme would have been as easy as the last two. The good thing about Turkey was that it wasn't involved in the war at all. Nazi Germany hadn't tried to take control of any of its regions and Turkey in response had not tried to fight on either side. This meant that even if they had to walk, they wouldn't be at risk at all.

They walked out onto the street. They saw cars, bikes and horse-drawn carriages which scattered lazily on both sides of the roads, almost like there were no driving rules. Boone attempted to talk to a few of the people who were driving cars. His Turkish was a bit rusty compared to other languages. Not to say he didn't know the language, as he did perfectly. The problem was most people still didn't take kind to people who sounded like they were from elsewhere in the world.

After only an hour of talking with drivers through their windows, they decided that the walk to Göreme may be their only option. So that's what they did. Driving would have placed them there in just over an hour; walking however, meant they were in for a solid twenty hour walk. Mary-Ann complained a little about her legs or how long the journey had taken to this point. Boone knew that he'd left out so many details from her about what was going to happen here. If she had known everything, she wouldn't have minded the extra time walking together. This meant, on the other hand, Boone enjoyed the idea of spending this next day with Mary-Ann still by his side, talking, laughing and hearing stories.

This hope, or luck, depending on whose side you're on, was cut short. Only ten minutes into their twenty-hour journey they heard the slow rhythmic sound of horses' feet walking towards them. They pulled off to the side of the road to avoid being hit before it pulled up beside them.

"Seer Mary-Ann, your presence has been sought."

Boone and Mary-Ann instantly turned their heads towards the voice coming from next to them. They looked up at a boy sitting at the front of a wheeled carriage being pulled by a single horse. They both looked puzzled at each other, then back to the boy.

The boy was young, early to mid-teens. He wore a brown robe, which had a hood pulled over his head and a tanned rope which hooked around his waist and pulled tight. He didn't repeat his words but carried on looking at Mary-Ann, not even taking a second glance at Boone.

"Wh... what?" Mary-Ann said.

"Your presence has been sought. Please come with me."

"By whom?" Boone interjected.

This was when the boy turned his head to Boone and looked at him in shock, almost like before now he was completely invisible to him.

"Who are you?" The boy said.

"Basileios..."

The boy looked up, almost trying to remember if he had a second passenger he was meant to be picking up.

"Just Seer Mary-Ann."

"She is not leaving with you unless I am accompanying her." Boone said in a sterner voice.

"As God wills."

Boone couldn't stop shaking his head. He knew that Mary-Ann had been summoned to Seer Theron. He also knew that this was either some kind of test for Boone, or what Theron would call a practical joke. Nevertheless, they climbed up onto the carriage and before they even sat down; the carriage started moving again. They were on their way and they would both see Theron when they got there.

The boy who was leading the horse didn't say another single thing to his passengers as the time slowly counted down. It would have only taken them two hours by horse-drawn carriage if it wasn't for the boy slowing down every five minutes to allow the horse to stop and smell the flowers along the way. It was like time didn't exist at the same rate for everyone.

The town of Göreme was both familiar and unknown to Boone. Like he'd stepped into a dream, but everything that should be there wasn't and everything that is there, looks wrong.

They trotted through the main streets and past sideroads. Everywhere they looked, they would see the same rock formation spire over and over again, created by the earth millions of years ago. These rock formations would serve as the homes, churches and monasteries to those who lived there. Carved by people in the fourth century, these came to be known as fairy chimneys.

The boy led the horse to a smaller rock spire, which was at the base of a mountain. It didn't look familiar to Boone, so wasn't exactly sure what to expect who or may be there. The boy hopped down from the carriage, secured the horse to a post and simply walked back towards the town without saying a single word. Both Boone and Mary-Ann looked at each other with confusion.

"Looks like he and the rocks have the same personality", Boone said to Mary-Ann as he looked back towards the spire.

The doorway on the spire creaked loudly as it opened up to an old man coming through to greet them. He looked to be bordering on 100 years old. A bald head pointed towards them as the man's back hunched over at a thirty-degree angle towards them. He shuffled his feet towards them, barely making an impact on the distance he needed to cover. The brown robes hovered just above the ground as his sandaled feet made millimetres of movements.

They both watched him as he slowly crept towards them. He stopped barely more than two feet from his front door and cranked his head up to look at them.

"How long are we going to do this! You have perfectly working legs, Seer Mary-Ann, don't make an old man walk all that way."

The man's voice was stoic, but a little higher than you would have expected but it was still loud as he yelled across to them both.

Mary-Ann quickly made her way to the man and stood in front of him. He arched up his body so he was facing towards her head, looking her in the eyes. He scanned back down from her shoulders and down her arms towards her legs then her feet.

"It'll do. Follow me."

He didn't look back at Boone; in fact, he didn't even acknowledge he existed. Boone shook his head once again as Theron turned and shuffled back inside, Mary-Ann following closely behind.

The inside of his home was small, but had everything needed for a single older man. It consisted mostly of a bed, a kitchen and a small sitting area with two seats to which he instructed Mary-Ann to go sit down.

"Theron", Boone said, trying to get his attention.

Theron looked up towards Boone for the first time and looked him up and down.

"Basileios", Theron said in shock. He stared at him almost like he was trying to come up with a long-forgotten memory.

"You are still here. I thought you were leaving for Engla land?" He recanted.

"England, Theron, it's been called that for centuries. Also, I moved there over six hundred years ago." Boone said in shock.

"Yes, of course. Anyway, fetch two teas for Seer Mary-Ann and myself."

"Unbelievable", Boone whispered under his breath as he went towards the kitchen.

Five minutes later, Boone returned from the kitchen and sat two teas down for both Theron and Mary-Ann. Theron looked at the cup, then lifted his head to look Boone in the eyes.

"Basileios... what are you doing here? You've gotten fat!"

Mary-Ann stifled a laugh as she both looked amused and shocked at the same time. Boone released a long, breathy sigh.

"You've gone mad, Theron."

He placed a hand on the head of Theron and shut his eyes. To Mary-Ann, the sight of what was happening right in front of her was nothing more than exactly that. She didn't see the flow of energy as it transferred from one life to another. She didn't notice the slight, subtle changes in the way Theron's spine uncurled itself and his eyes appeared wider and more clear. In contrast, it wasn't until Boone had pulled his hand away from Theron's head that she looked towards him and noticed her friend, her father figure, her master now standing there, as an old man.

Theron jolted up from his seat with a newfound energy and stronger bones.

"Basileios, you shouldn't have done that." His voice sounded deeper and clearer than he was only a moment ago. "I need to give you some back."

"No. I will be fine. I'll get it back over time. You were losing your mind, old man."

Theron laughed and wrapped his arms around Boone in a way that said, 'It's nice to see you' and gave him a kiss on the cheek.

Theron turned towards Mary-Ann. "This! A marvellous change to the world. A new seer!"

❧

The next few days flowed like six centuries hadn't just passed since being in Göreme. Boone was able to show Mary-Ann around the places with which he once held a connection and shared the emotional memories that came with them. They spent the nights together cooking, laughing and learning about each other's lives. Boone knew the truth that she was only days away from starting her training as a Seer and that meant him leaving. Potentially not seeing her for a very long time. He wasn't sure how he felt about this. It had been a long time since he'd felt a familial bond with anyone; he didn't want to lose her now but knew it would be for the best. Her existence in this world was far greater than recent Soul Keepers before her or after.

"Has Theron let you know what you will be learning?" Boone enquired one morning.

Mary-Ann bobbed her head from side to side as she peeled an orange. This was her way of saying, 'Kind of, but not really.'

"All I know is that he said we will be leaving soon. But I'm not sure where. Oh, he also said I'm not meant to tell anyone about my Keeps... ever. I have to keep who I take an absolute secret, even from him and you! Can you believe that?"

Boone sat back in his seat and contemplated for a while. He knew the life of a Seer better than anyone else who wasn't one. He knew the secrets they had to keep and why they had to keep them. He felt it was important to tell her some things now, rather than her trying to listen to the riddles from Theron.

"You will be the Keeper of Keepers. You will take the souls of not only those in the world around us, but you will take the souls of those who we love, our children, our wives and husbands. You will know when and roughly where these people will die. You are sworn to a secret so big that the world could be flipped upside down if one of those Keeps are saved."

"We, even as Soul Keepers, do have an end. You already know mine."

Boone fell into the habit of worrying himself more than he needed to. He spent more nights stirring in his sleep as he thought about what the future might hold for Mary-Ann. He worried about her safety; making sure she was well fed, thriving and alive. He knew that Theron would never do anything to her that could potentially be harmful to her life, but he also knew the tests and trials that she would be put through. A lot of these would almost make her feel like she was about to die.

He took solace in the fact that Theron, as a Seer himself, could see her death day. Vice versa, Mary-Ann could also see Theron's death day. Boone would quite often observe the shock every time she saw Theron walking into the room. The nervousness she felt when she was around him. Not because of the person who he was, but Boone thought it might be because of his date of death. Almost like she wanted to or needed to talk to somebody about it.

Chapter Twenty Five

A knock on the door rang out in the quiet moonlit night. The rapping on the door echoed through the entire room like some kind of wake up chant from the beyond. Quiet, barefooted steps were heard as Boone peeled back the blankets, preparing to leap up from his prone body and attack the very thing which had intruded the night for himself and Mary-Ann.

He opened his eyes and stared into the darkness. It was Theron. He was standing alongside the bed of Mary-Ann, whispering into her ear with her nodding along to his every word. Boone looked at the clock which read four am on the dot.

"You have five minutes and we will be leaving; prepare yourself." Theron said as he walked towards the open door.

"How long will she be gone?" Boone interjected.

Theron turned towards Boone with a questioning look. "You know better than to ask that, young mathetes."

They both climbed out of bed. Boone watched Mary-Ann as she paced around the room, grabbing this and that, packing her clothes into a bag and taking little trinkets they'd found over time. She took quick glances over to Boone, the look on her face begging for some kind of reassurance. He struggled to give that to her.

Theron was outside on the horse-drawn carriage that waited for Mary-Ann. They now stood at the doorway of the room, barely able to come up with anything to say to each other now, after everything. She reached her arms around Boone and held him tight.

"Thank you, Boethius."

Tears came to her eyes and, without taking a second look at him, she turned and walked towards Theron.

Theron clicked his mouth and the horse moved forward and away into the moonlit night.

Boone knew he had done the right thing by bringing her here. But the regret flowed through him like hot lava through his veins. He regretted every moment of the trek that brought them to Turkey. He hated that she had to leave or that he couldn't go with her. He felt useless and lost, like he was losing a daughter all over again.

ॐ

Boone didn't leave Theron's spire house that night, nor the next, or the one after that. He spent each night waking up every few hours and looking into the moonlight, wondering if the noise he heard was of their returning. Or every day hearing the galloping feet of horses on the roads, expecting the sight of Mary-Ann returning home. Back to the house that he was now living in.

Those days turned into weeks and the weeks into months. Eventually, the world had taken its journey around the sun and the anniversary date of when she had left had arrived. He knew he couldn't wait here forever. The souls that he was to Keep were getting less and less in the area and he needed to move onto somewhere new. He knew that at this current rate, he could still live a relatively long life, even at the human age he was now.

Boone packed his belongings into a bag, found an old gold cache of his in the area and left.

It was 1942. Turkey was still avoiding any conflict to do with the war, so travelling still wasn't an issue. He made his way north back towards Ankara where he rented a small apartment in the middle of the city. The apartment was small, only barely enough for one person. It was on the fourth floor of a four story building which overlooked another line of identical brick buildings.

A month went by and he ended up getting a part-time job as a teacher at one of the close by high schools. He enjoyed the distraction that the kids would give him. He saw the good and the bad, the worthy of more and the soon to be dropouts. Souls were keeping him busy both during the day and night. He gained more internal life energy with every soul he took, which he put half towards improving his age slightly and the other half to hidden reserves.

Three months in, he purchased an American imported car called a Ford Duluxe. He had heard of the brand of car and may have even noticed one or two in the UK, but never had the need or want for one before now. His first trip in his new car was back down to Göreme to see if Mary-Ann or Theron had made any return home. He found they had not. He turned around and went straight back to Ankara.

Boone would repeat this cycle of driving back to Göreme every two to three months. He'd check Theron's home, local restaurants or spots where he himself had trained in the past, but nothing. There were no hints that he could take from any of it.

Those months stretched from two to three, three to four and four to five. Eventually, he only returned every six months.

Each year that passed was easier than the one before that. Memories, although always there, started to fade as the feeling of loss started to get easier.

Before he knew it, ten years had passed.

The world felt different now. The war was over and a lot of the countries that had fought seemed to be working together. Twelve Western countries that were part of the war formed something called NATO, which was in an aim to counter the Soviet threat. Even Italy joined NATO in the end, with talks of Germany soon to follow. It felt calmer and safer out there, not that Boone had travelled outside of Turkey for any of that.

"Do you have any schoolwork to grade tonight?"

Boone looked up from the cutting board and beyond the bench top.

"Not tonight, hun."

The woman in front of him nodded and carried on reading the book she had placed in front of her. She licked her lips just before sliding a small cherry tomato between them, accentuating her feminine appeal. Her long black hair fell to her face as she moved it and tucked it behind her ear once more.

"Sofija, I'll be heading down to Göreme this Saturday. Would you like to come?"

Sofija looked up from her book in surprise, trying not to show too much enthusiasm.

She slightly smiled, "You've never asked me to come before. In the two years that we have been together, you've always said that you had to do it alone."

Boone slowly nodded. Part of him knew it was going to be another uninformative trip, but still hoped for the best. He hadn't exactly told her anything about his real life, but she knew there was something different about him. Those little trips to the city in the middle of the night or the random drives out to seemingly random locations made her question him for a start. Eventually came to pass that he was just different.

He was right once again. The trip down to Göreme turned up nothing new. By now, Boone mostly stopped by for only a few minutes just to check on Theron's home and then leave.

It had been decades since Boone had enjoyed the company of a woman, but Sofija seemed to slide into his life so simply and so easily, like she had always been there. They met at a local bakery. It wasn't a one day, love at first sight kind of meeting. It was a small, friendly smile that flew between them as they passed each other every day for a week. That small friendly smile turned into a devilish cheeky smile from Sofija and then eventually after a few weeks, Boone introduced himself.

They flirted back and forth over the next two days. Without even realising it, they were six dates deep and seemed to be enjoying each other's company more than their own. Now, two years in, they no longer tried to keep up with the amount of dates they had been on. In fact, Sofija spent at least half of her nights now with Boone and the other half back home.

Time passed easily these days as another six months clocked over with Boone making his trip down to Göreme and then returning home. He walked into his apartment in Ankara to find Sofija reading a book, snacking on fruit as she sat in the sun beaming in through the window. She smiled and tilted her head up as he passed her and gave her a slow and loving peck on the lips.

"How was your trip?" She asked.

He opened his mouth to answer, but just before he had the chance, he felt the presence of someone attempting to find him. Within a second, he knew who it was and allowed the connection to happen.

Theron phased into existence right in front of Boone.

"Hello Basileios, we are home."

He phased out.

A man of many words, Boone thought to himself.

"Hun, I have to go back."

Sofija put down her book. "You just got back? I assume you didn't find what you were looking for and came back. What makes you think it'll be any different now?"

"I can't explain. I have to go."

He grabbed his keys once more, gave her another kiss and ran out the door and was off down the road.

Twelve years. Will she even remember me? What will she look like now? What will she think of me, just sitting around doing nothing all day?

Thoughts plagued Boone's mind as the road between him and Göreme seemed to grow longer than he had ever seen it before. The whole time she was gone, he worried about her safety and the fact that she had gone and now he was alone. It had only clicked to him just now that she may have been feeling the same way. Alone with Theron, Boone gone and no one to talk to or laugh with.

Four hours later, Boone crawled his car along the last remaining dirt road and stopped less than fifty metres from Theron's house. He climbed out of the car and stood, breathing in the air with a deep breath as he looked towards the home which he'd seen as empty for over a decade.

A loud BANG echoed out through the cool air as the front door to the home flung open and Boone saw Mary-Ann sprinting for him faster than he'd ever seen her before. Without saying a word, she opened her arms and jumped towards him with an embrace, not letting go for five minutes.

"Hi", she said eventually.

"Hello, Mary-Ann."

She tore herself away from him and he could see that her eyes were red with tears as they stood staring at each other.

A yell came from the front door of the house, "She is much easier to train than you were, Basileios and you were almost 500 years old by the time we met!"

Boone raised his hand to Theron to say a solemn thank you while Mary-Ann laughed as they both headed towards the house.

The conversation from Theron was to be expected. He let Boone know the very basics of where they had been and what they had been doing over the last twelve years. This, of course, wasn't unusual for Theron. Boone knew him well and remembered his own training throughout the years. Although different from what a Seer might have learnt, he assumed it was mostly the same.

One of the good pieces of news that came out of that night was that Mary-Ann had finished her training and was allowed to leave. It took her only twelve years what Boone had learnt in fifteen. He was proud of her, like any father would be.

The next day came and they drove back up to Ankara. Boone told Mary-Ann the stories of his last decade. Getting an apartment, a car and a job. He bragged about Sofija and about their years together. He could feel that Mary-Ann was mostly silent, listening to the stories but itching to tell her own. Her eyebrows would raise, then fall, pitch then flatten as her own thoughts banged on the inside of her mind to say something out loud. She was of course sworn to secrecy.

"Can I tell you one thing?" She asked with a smile.

"You can tell me whatever you like. Your secrecy is not your honour; it isn't to protect you, it is to protect others. If you feel it's safe to tell me something, then so be it."

Mary-Ann nodded at this. It is something that Theron would have drilled into her hard over the years. The reason for her existing. The reason for her receiving this role from the universe.

"I'm no longer in pain. I no longer hear the vibration that used to drill into my head twenty-four hours a day. Theron was able to help me meditate and now I can close off the world around me without even closing my eyes."

"That is great, Mary-Ann. Are you still seeing ripples?"

"Yes. I see the ripples through the air. But they've never been the issue."

The drive back to Ankara felt quicker this time, like time flew faster than ever before. They climbed up the eight flights of stairs to get to Boone's apartment, opened the front door and stepped in to see Sofija standing in the kitchen staring back at them both.

Boone had a giant smile on his face while he looked at Sofija, like he just woke up on Christmas morning and saw the Christmas tree had gifts under it.

"Mary-Ann, this is Sofija."

"Sofija, this is Mary-Ann, my..."

Boone didn't know what to say. He didn't want to say friend; that didn't give enough weight to the relationship and the times they had spent together. She wasn't his daughter, not truly, so couldn't introduce her as that either.

"She is my family."

Sofija smiled politely at Mary-Ann and came over to give her a hug. Boone had talked about Mary-Ann from time to time, but he did it in a way that made her sound young and helpless. To Sofija, this was a beautiful girl in her mid thirties.

Sofija wasn't one to be jealous at all. She was, however, confused about who and what Mary-Ann turned out to be. Sofija was from Slovenia and had only just moved to Turkey a few years back. Her accent wasn't heavy to Boone anymore. But he knew that when the accent got heavier, it's because her brain focused on other thoughts and processes rather than sounding like she wasn't an outsider.

Sofija herself was in the middle of her forties with Boone leading ahead with his human age of roughly fifty-two.

"I'm sorry for my confusion, Mary-Ann. The way Boone talked about you suggested that you were much younger and more of a daughter to him than anything else. But you two aren't as far apart in age as I thought you were going to be."

"Guess I need to work on my skincare." Mary-Ann said with a laugh, trying to avoid the topic of aging.

"I guess I need to get a bigger apartment now." Boone said.

Mary-Ann put her head down slightly, almost ashamed of what she was about to say.

"Boone... I actually can't stay for long."

Silence followed.

"Oh", Boone said finally.

Chapter Twenty six

"Long" was the key word in the sentence which Mary-Ann had just sprung on Boone. He knew that if he had taken even more than one minute to sit and think about who she is now, he would have realised she wouldn't be able to stay still and just bask in the city life-style like he did.

Boone knew what it was like being a new Soul Keeper. He knew the late nights trying to perfect the ultimate capture of souls. He knew the waiting and watching of people as their shadows danced around their homes like a never ending puppet show. He'd spent countless days and nights soul stalking one individual after another as the years trickled on. Of course, as he got older and wiser, he knew the signs of people exiting their homes. He also knew when to put on that gas company uniform or pick the right flowers to become the florist delivery man.

Mary-Ann did in fact leave only after a couple of days at the Ankara apartment. As her secret life began, Boones carried on once more as he had been. He didn't mind one bit now. He knew that Mary-Ann was safe; he had Sofija and he was starting to think of Ankara as his home. At this point in his life, he wished nothing would change.

That wish would come true, they didn't change.

The years ticked over. Mary-Ann would return to Boone and Sofija every special holiday or birthday. She'd stop by on rare occasions where her Keeps would put her within a short driving or walking distance to Ankara. Sofija ended up adoring Mary-Ann. She looked forward to her visits almost as much as Boone did.

Each year that passed felt faster than the one before that. In the first thousand years that Boone had lived, he felt like barely anything changed from one year to the next. The same people worked in the same fields. The cities grew, but at such a small rate that you wouldn't have even known it.

The late 1950s were moving fast to Boone. The new music that was coming out was vastly different from he had ever heard before. Elvis and Buddy Holly had taken over the world of music and even Boone couldn't help himself but shake a leg before pulling up Sofija into a full on swinging dance. Household televisions were getting more and more popular as sci-fi movies would play on the big screens in the middle of the city. One of the big things for him was the USSR launching Sputnik into space as the very first space satellite.

Boone had given up on trying to work out why he or other Soul Keepers had been given these roles in the world. He had once believed in the gods, believing that he was chosen to act as that connection between heaven and earth. The satellite that went to space made him think. He thought about the possibility of it finding something that had never been seen before. Maybe it would uncover the world's mysteries. Maybe, just maybe, it would give him an answer that, although he had forgotten about, he had been searching all his life for.

1961 and 1962 crossed with what felt like the world was more separated than ever. Wars were starting everywhere and everything seemed to be a competition for the first country to do one thing or another. Boone had seen these kinds of things play out over time but on a slower scale. After World War Two, everyone seemed to be afraid of the next time nuclear weapons were to be used. Everyone would talk about the idea of leaving one country for the next, thinking it'd be safer.

The life of the rest of the world didn't affect any major changes in Boone or Sofija's life. They carried on living as they had for the previous nine years and were almost about to celebrate their tenth year together.

"Mary-Ann called while you were at work." Sofija mentioned as they sat in the courtyard.

"Oh? Where is she now? Did she mention when she'd be back? It's coming up Christmas and I thought it might be soon."

"Mhmm, she's in Estonia. She said she's on her way back by train and she's got something important she needs to ask."

Once December rolled around, Mary-Ann ended up coming down via train to see Boone. She looked both tougher than he'd seen her before, but also still like the young girl he once knew her as.

"Hey Boone!" She yelled as she skipped up the steps to the apartment on the fourth floor.

"I could sense you coming. Thought I'd get off my arse and meet you at the door."

She gave him a kiss on the cheek before flopping down onto the couch inside like a limp fish.

"So! You are my guide! I remember you said that to me once. I know Theron is my master, but you are my guide... right?"

"I am, but you've never really needed me. You came to me at such a busy time for both of us. I guess you're wanting something."

"Pocket money?" Boone said jokingly to Mary-Ann, giving her a wink.

Just then, Sofija entered the apartment carrying a brown paper bag of vegetables.

"Money? Mary-Ann do you need money?"

"No, Sofija! Boone was just teasing."

Mary-Ann put her head down, now suddenly having second thoughts about the question and conversation she was about to have with Boone. She shuffled her feet as though she was still a school student asking her father if she could go to a friend's house.

"I need to leave... probably for good."

She waited and watched as the weight of the words fell upon Boone and Sofija. She didn't want to leave, but as part of her role, she had to, but didn't want to go alone.

"Okay..." Boone said, "How long do we have to pack?"

"Boone!" Sofija yelled.

Mary-Ann's heart beat faster as the realisation of what might happen could have effects that reached beyond herself and Boone. She knew Sofija and Boone had been together for ten years now. She could see that Boone didn't heal one day of that and if he had it any other way, he would grow old with her.

"Sofija, I love you and you know I want to spend the rest of our lives together if I could."

Boone stopped mid-thought. He looked at Mary-Ann and then back at Sofija.

"I have to tell you something", he said slowly.

The mumbled conversation from Boone and Sofija's room lasted from sundown, all the way through the night and way into the next day. Mary-Ann could hear the shallow words that escaped Boone's mouth. The almost silent tears that wept from Sofija as she moved from denial to acceptance and then the final words of love, desire and longing which had kept them together for so long already.

They exited the room in the afternoon the next day to Mary-Ann buttering some toast and half shovelling it into her mouth. Sofija looked at Mary-Ann with a crooked head, almost like a dog would if it heard an odd sound that interested it.

"You are... a Seer", Sofija said slowly.

Mary-Ann choked and then nodded, almost afraid of breaking her silent vows.

"Sofija will join us wherever we are going... Where are we going, Mary-Ann?"

With Mary-Ann's world surrounded by the secrets of being a Seer, Boone knew that she wouldn't have been able to tell them much. He, of course, could surmise that she needed to leave for a country for a high-profile target. A soul that needed to be kept. More than likely, another Soul Keeper.

Boone, with the help of Stuart, was able to obtain another fake passport and leave with Mary-Ann and Sofija for the other side of the world.

It took them four days of crossing country after country where the planes would refuel and restock. They eventually landed in their new home in New Zealand.

The city was different. Much greener and more natural than the city of Ankara or even the city of London. It felt new, like everyone had just been placed here and they were all wandering around wondering what to do next or build next.

Boone immediately bought a place just outside the metro area of the city. A nice four-bedroom home that was perfect for Boone, Mary-Ann and Sofija to all fit in perfectly, which they did.

Boone immediately started to get souls he needed to Keep. Spending days and nights scouring the streets looking for information or clues as to how he could speed his soul taking up or make it easier. Things like what the local police or firemen look like. How easy would it be to move through the city without a car or by simply walking. He was starting a new life and wanted this one to be as easy as possible.

Sofija also started working at a local school named the Avondale Primary School. She enjoyed the work and particularly enjoyed the kids and watching them laugh and play. She knew from her conversation with Boone why they couldn't have their own kids and had accepted that in the short time they'd started living in Avondale.

She would quite often see the kids out and about at the shops or parks being watched over by their parents. It was one of Sofija and Boone's favourite pass-times to just sit in the gardens and watch over the world as it moved on by. It wasn't uncommon for the parents with their kids to come over to Sofija and say hello. There was one child in particular who was so adamant about saying hi to his teacher that he dragged his mother over to Sofija.

"Hey Mrs Stone!"

Sofija smiled and gave him a little wave.

"Sorry, Mrs Stone." The mother said. "He was so concerned at not getting to come over and say hello, I just had to bring him over."

The boy barely looked at Sofija as they talked. Instead, he had his eyes firmly placed upon Boone.

"Oh, I'm so sorry." Sofija said. "This is my partner, Boone. Boone, this is Catherine and her little boy, Scott, Scott Wilson."

Scott beamed a wide grinned smile at Boone. "Hello Mister."

Sofija and Catherine carried on talking together, completely ignoring the odd silence that lingered after the 'Hello' that Scott had given. Boone looked at the boy and into his eyes.

"Hello, Scott Wilson." Boone reached out to shake the five-year-old boy's hand. "My name is Boethius; I will be your guide."

Chapter Twenty Seven

Scott Wilson was a good kid in primary school. He listened to his teachers, did his work in silence and never complained about how hard anything was, no matter the subject. He took an early interest in technology, hardware and all the flashing lights and dials that came with it. To Scott, life was packed full of capacitors, diodes, wires and plugs. Anything that contained either a battery or was plugged into the wall outlet was examined. The toaster's fiery innards, the remote-control car's battery pack, those slots that ran down the back of the TV in the corner of the living room. Each and every one of them was like looking into another universe of mazes.

It wasn't until he started taking them apart that he eventually led himself to get in trouble. Of course, he'd never put them back together again. At least not in the correct way.

As he grew older, more of that obsession became apparent. He'd fall into a rhythm of focusing one thing, mastering that, then moving on to the next. First, spending time on it, examining it and seeing how it turned on and off, how it got its power and what its seemingly magical abilities were behind it. Second, take it apart. A lamp on a table turned into a heap of wires and an odd-looking vase. A walkie-talkie turned into a pile of capacitors and resistors, barely resembling what it once had been.

By the time he was a teenager, he would sacrifice sleep just to stay up all night reading magazines about computer parts and new technology. He had heard about these guys over in California, USA, creating new, amazing personal computers from their garage. He dreamt about doing the same thing, creating something with his bare hands and sharing it with the world, getting praise where he wasn't getting it now.

Scott did dream of this, but he also dreamed about money and stardom. He dreamed of being better than the next person and never backing down from a fight. He wanted to be the best, no matter who he had to take down.

At twenty years old in 1978, he joined another group of misfits who filled in the gaps that he was missing. He learnt how to hack and how to fix gambling machines to spit out payouts at just the right time. Just enough so that he wouldn't get caught and no attention would be brought to him. He rigged automatic teller machines to hold on to people's cash just long enough that they would walk away and he would return for his payday.

Scott had always felt like he didn't fit in this world in one way or another. He had felt since childhood that things didn't always make sense. Those days would change from a sunny day to a loud thunderous roar and then back again. Like he had just lived three days all within one hour. As he got older, his concern grew about his health. He would visit doctors, psychologists, priests, his parents and sometimes even question the gods as to why he could be completely fine one moment and the next moment, a dying sickness would plague his body.

When he turned twenty-one, that year, everything almost came to a crashing halt.

June nights are often cold. Often dark and stormy on occasion. A night turning from just that to even more of a dull, gloomy night wasn't anything that would be noticed, no matter the person. There was one particular night in June that Scott will remember for the rest of his life. It started out like any of the other hundred nights before that.

"Scott! Dude! You should see the game Paul just brought in today!" Mark said.

"It's nothing. I just created a game for the PET. It's like, you go through this maze until you find the exit and then once it's found, you get presented with a nice pair of tits on the screen! All up in your face!"

Paul cupped an imaginary pair of breasts on his chest as he walked slowly towards Scott, swinging his hips from side to side.

"Cut it out, dude!" Scott yelled as he laughed and swatted away Paul.

The night was early, but the skies were dark and cloudy. Not that they had a window to look at in the basement they were in, but if they were to look out of one, they would have seen no stars or moon at all in the sky.

A sudden cold whipped through the basement as they all clattered away on their computers. Scott looked around at the others who didn't seem to notice the temperature change. He shook it off and put his head down again. He was working on a new code to slow down the gates at the races, giving one horse in particular an advantage of a quick getaway and leaving the others behind.

A few hours into the night, the basement still had Scott, Paul, Mark and half a dozen of their other friends all working away, laughing and drinking alcohol. There was nothing overtly different about the night, but Scott could just tell something was weird. He had stopped drinking his beer an hour before that and decided now would be a good time to get up and grab a coffee.

Just as Scott stood up to grab a coffee, a loud rumbling sounded from outside. It was getting louder and louder until it was eventually noticeable that it was a vehicle that had cut its engine just outside the basement.

Weird... Scott thought to himself. Everyone seems to be here tonight. I don't know who that would be.

He shook his head and looked around at his crew. Everyone else at this point was wearing headphones and had either some game playing in their ears or music pumping so loud they wouldn't be able to hear a thing. Scott was the only one who heard the loud footsteps of someone coming down the basement stairs.

The door swung open with an icy breeze blasting through. It slammed into the wall inside and sent a shockwave through the desks. Everyone looked up and towards the man now standing at the doorway. No one moved.

The man, who looked like some kind of enormous Terminator replica scanned the room. He wore black from head to toe, including an unfortunate balaclava, which told everyone in that room what he was there for.

Scott's mind raced as his eyes flew down towards the man's hands, which held a rifle.

Gun

Looks like .303 Lee-Enfield...

Seven point seven by fifty-six mm powdered cartridge. Rear-locking, bolt-action.

Barrel steel... stocks... Walnut? Maybe Beechwood.

Magazine is... what, ten in the mag, double stacked. That's twenty to thirty rounds per minute.

It's loud; people will hear it. He doesn't care; he has a mask.

BANG BANG

Scott's world slowed down to what almost felt like it stopped completely. The sound of gunfire passed him like it was giving him every moment in the world to stop and examine it. The problem was he couldn't move.

Time caught up with him and he spun his head around with just enough time to see Mark's head split open as though someone had thrown a can of tomato sauce at him. Scott's eyes grew wide as his mind finally caught on to what was happening. Someone was here to kill Mark.

Another two shots went off and hit another one of his friends, Brendon. His body now also lay lifeless on the ground alongside Mark. The remaining people in the room had now ducked and covered out of the way of any immediate gunfire, apart from Scott.

He was frozen. His senses knew he was in danger but he had never actually come to face anything even nearly like this. He remained in the middle of the room, completely facing the man in black alone, but unwillingly.

The man turned the barrel of the gun towards Scott. He lifted his hand towards the man like he was somehow going to block any oncoming fire that was about to come his way.

"No, wait!"

The man pulled the trigger. The bullet flew through the air, into Scott's hand and out the other side. With no time to even contemplate his life, the bullet entered his forehead, all in less than half a second.

Chapter Twenty Eight

"Ahhh!"

Scott's scream to his own head felt like he was coming out of a tunnel, going from one end to another while the echo's reverberated around until they found their way back to his ears. To the others around him, the scream made no sense and was completely random.

A small crowd full of heads turned towards Scott as he stood, lanky, in the middle of the room as though he was the centre of a carousel. He looked from face to face, almost about to yell to everyone to get down and hide. That was until he realised everyone looked calm and normal. His hands immediately went up to his forehead, searching for a hole that did not exist and blood that did not slip between his fingers.

"What the hell just happened?" He said out loud, as though someone could read his mind.

The room of on-lookers were Scott's friends. He'd known them all for years now, but no one made a peep; it was silent. Scott would have sworn that the world slowed down again until a loud rattling came from someone just outside the basement door. Scott turned his head in shock towards the door, knowing what was about to happen.

The handle turned and Scott once again froze in place. His heart raced and breathing became uncontrollable as his chest grew and fell at an alarming rate. The door slowly opened and Scott squinted his eyes, expecting to see the unknown man who had just taken his life once already.

"Taxi?" Boone hung his head in the door and yelled to the room. "Did anyone order a taxi?"

"N... No... Nobody", Scott stammered.

Just behind Boone, Mary-Ann walked in all confidently. "Are you sure?" She asked.

She went to Mark and laid her hand on his shoulder gently. "Did you? Order a taxi?"

"Uh, no", he replied. "But I'll go wherever you're going."

Mary-Ann looked at the smirk on Mark's face and gave him a teasing smile before walking to the next person. She went to five of the men in the basement, touching them while asking if they had ordered a taxi.

No one else in the room moved. They all just stayed silent, watching as Mary-Ann made her way around the room.

Boone pulled a note from his pocket. "This taxi has been booked for Scott Wilson."

Boone looked around the room pretending he didn't know who Scott looked like. It had been fifteen years since they had met each other. To Scott, he didn't remember that meeting. He was young and although Boone could see who he was, he wouldn't need to be guided or trained until much later. Of course, Boone knew exactly what Scott looked like. He had been keeping an eye on him every single week for years now. Making sure that he would know when the time was right and when he needed to interject himself into his life.

"M... me?" Scott stammered again.

"Yes, Scott. Come with us."

Mary-Ann reached around Scott's left arm, almost as though he was about to lead her onto the dance floor and slow dance the whole night. She smiled a sympathetic smile at him and slowly walked him out of the room with Boone instead.

"I think I have to stay..." Scott mentioned to Boone without giving him a reason why.

Scott had a big personality on him at most times. He was never afraid to say what he thought and never backed down from something which may be a challenge. In this moment, he acted young, very young. He was unsure and confused. Of course, this was to be expected after seeing something that didn't completely make sense.

"I know you feel that way, Scott. I'm sorry for your loss. This will be one of the worst nights of your life", Mary-Ann interjected.

"Who are you?" He said.

"My name is Mary-Ann and this is Boethius. You can call him Boone."

Boone turned towards Scott, wondering if there would be any sign of recognition. There wasn't. It had been fifteen years, so for anyone to remember a name and a face from that time and never see them again would be a challenge. For a child, it might as well have been hard for that memory to last more than a minute.

They were only three hundred metres down the street and a set of gun blasts rang out over the empty roads, echoing through the darkness.

"Wait... No!"

Scott started to run back towards the basement like he was escaping from two prison guards. They weren't holding him and Boone knew through foresight that this would happen. He expected it and let it happen anyway. The point of taking Scott from that room was not to save him from the mental damage of seeing his friends die. The point was that the universe didn't want him to save them.

Boone and Mary-Ann stared at each other with knowing faces and started walking back in the direction of the basement.

The eerie silence dawned down upon the 19 Lockwood Street basement. Scott, with Mary-Ann and Boone standing behind him, looked into the room of death. Boone and Mary-Ann with sorrow filled hearts that never change and then Scott, with nothing but shock and disbelief.

The strew of bodies lay wildly placed on the floors, slumped over desks and one even looked calmly normal sitting on a sofa at the back of the room. Blood filled so much of the floor and walls of the room, it looked like there had been some kind of chemical spill of red dye.

Boone knew what the next thoughts going through Scott's head would be; what, why, how and then the last, who are you?

"What happened? I don't understand? Why do I... I've... How... I should be dead."

Boone raised his eyebrows with his only little shocked surprise to have been correct, but almost not, at the same time.

"I was here and I died", Scott said, slowly lifting his hand again to his forehead.

A completely normal sentence to a Soul Keeper. Not so much to anyone else.

Scott turned towards Boone, looking for an answer and paused. He looked over Boone's shoulder and to the other side of the street.

Boone turned to look and saw the shining glow of Selene. Her blonde hair and white sun dress illuminating the dark street around her.

"What is that? Is that an angel?" Scott asked.

Boone smiled. "I think you should go talk with her."

Chapter Twenty Nine

Destiny, fate, calling, ordained path; whatever you want to call it, it happens if we like it or not. Being a Soul Keeper gives people the ability to see into the future either a few minutes or in Mary-Ann's case, days, weeks or even years. Theron had honed her abilities in the decade long training he bore down on her day after day with no day off between.

Mary-Ann's heart and head were in a constant battle between good and evil. She knew her own path; she had been given and the responsibility behind it. She knew that there were certain rules that she was given and for the most part; she followed those rules. This, however, she couldn't.

"Boone." She said.

It had been a year since Boone had taken on Scott and his Soul Keeper abilities. They would occasionally still watch him from a distance like two undercover police surveilling him while eating ham sandwiches in the front of their cruiser. They'd watch the tough jobs, the ones that required him to be sly or clever, to be fast or even agent-like. In this instance, nothing much was going on but they continued to watch.

Boone turned towards Mary-Ann. She was tough these days; the words that came out of her mouth were solid, forceful and direct. The subtle nervousness was obvious to him, almost like she'd just dyed her hair completely blue and was trying not to let anyone notice it.

"Yeah, Mary-Ann?"

"I have to tell you something, but... I don't know if I'm allowed."

Boone nodded. "You have your own rules you have chosen to follow. But, you're also given the sense to keep those rules as you see fit."

"Sofija will die soon."

Boone's breath was taken away from him like someone had just reached down his throat and squeezed his lungs. He fought internally with himself if he should be angry with Mary-Ann or thankful for her. Emotions played over in his head for thirty seconds without saying a single reply back to her.

"Thank you for letting me know."

Silence lingered in the air as they both carried on watching Scott stumble through a Soul collection.

"I... I didn't know if..."

"I know... Mary-Ann. That must have been difficult for you to bring up with me. Can you tell me when or even how?"

"Within six months... are you going to tell her?"

"How... Mary-Ann? How does it happen?"

"Cancer."

It had been almost two centuries since Boone had actually loved someone. He'd had relationships over that time, sometimes spending decades with some of them, others just passing friendships. He enjoyed his time with them, but never loved them. Sofija, he loved. Sofija was sixty-two at this stage, with Boone at the human age of around sixty-seven.

The choice he had to make wasn't should he try to heal her, but could he, was he allowed to?

Mary-Ann's souls that she collected were for a purpose. She often took the souls of the dying that if another Soul Keeper had been given the task, they would refuse. Sometimes, the future depended on the sacrifice of loved ones. How could you stop yourself from saving your son if he was dying, even if you knew that action would change the future, cause a butterfly effect and ten thousand other people would die? Most would still save the one they loved.

The same thoughts lingered between them both as they sat in the front of that car, ham sandwiches now ignored. Questions ran through both their heads. The moral dilemma of knowing the end but can't do anything about it or not realising the end was about to come and hating the person who took their soul.

"What would happen if I saved her?"

Mary-Ann slightly shrugged her shoulders. "I don't know. Two people die, three people die, the world ends?"

Boone turned to look at Mary-Ann to see if that was a joke. It wasn't. She truly didn't know what the actions of not collecting a soul for a seer would be.

A week later, Sofija broke the news to Boone about her cancer.

The next six months for Sofija and Boone were brutal. Sofija understood the position that Boone had been put in. She knew what Mary-Ann's position was. In the end, on that last quiet day, they all sat together and said their goodbyes. It was slow as Sofija took her last breaths in this world. Mary-Ann collected her soul only seconds before she passed.

Boone focused his senses in the room and now saw the soul of Sofija standing next to him, a smile plastered across her face.

"I feel like I've never felt this good."

Boone smiled gently. "You don't feel pain as a soul", he said softly.

Although they were an odd duo, they spent their last week together still as two loved ones, one being a soul. A week later, Sofija was lowered into her final resting place. She was gone.

Boone fell into a state of depression after her passing. He spent most days sitting at home staring out into space without a second glance at anyone around him. His beard grew long and the only time he got out into public was to take the soul of a few people per week.

He talked with Mary-Ann, but not in the way he used to. Most of the conversations would start off normal and then eventually get to a stage of life and death and then Sofija. He didn't hate the world or the responsibility of a Soul Keeper being forced upon him. He hated the fact that, as a Soul Keeper he didn't know what the next stage of life was. He would talk of the whispers in the Soul Keeper community of people who could slip between the realms of the living and that of the dead. But he had met no one of the kind, but felt like he knew they existed.

"They have to exist." He would complain. "Why would we be given this role as Soul Keepers just for them to go into the afterlife of nothingness?"

It made sense to Mary-Ann. She agreed, but was so young to being a Soul Keeper that she hadn't even thought about it, let alone heard the whispers.

A year after Sofija's death, James and Maggie Dunlop made their way over to New Zealand, finding a house and settling into their own life in the city of Avondale.

Dunlop made a conservative effort for Maggie to stay alive for as long as he could. She knew the risks of healing and knew from their long life together that there may be an end to it all. They were both prepared for that. James would give himself just enough to slow the aging process to where a ten years in a normal human would only equate to around one year for them both. This meant he could not help others ever again.

Dunlop became a police officer again with the idea of helping those in need as much as possible without using his Soul Keeper abilities. This also made it easier to get into homes or private areas when he needed to.

His being in Avondale had a huge impact on Boone. They talked with each other every day and eventually fell into their old friendship for the most part. There was still something lost about Boone that Dunlop saw every day.

With time comes healing. Every year that passed the memory started to fade of Sofija. He still loved her dearly and missed her every day of his life. He still had Mary-Ann and Dunlop to share his life with, but still felt like something was missing.

Time slipped away, bit by bit the memory of her had completely gone. Ten years had passed since he had lost her and all that had remained was doubt about the choice he had made and anger with the loss he had to take. He would constantly come back to the idea of there being a life after this one.

He'd repeat the same sentences over and over again like he was an Alzheimer's patient remembering he needed to pick up his dry cleaning from just down the road.

"There has to be something after this. Why do we help these people? Is it better for us, for them, for whoever this higher power is?"

Boone was older than both Mary-Ann and Dunlop combined, so they didn't have the answer for him.

He didn't want to just give up on this idea. He started to go down to the local park and sit under the trees and enter the void. He needed to talk to someone and that someone was Selene.

He spent a year doing this. Walking to the park, sitting down under the trees, closing his eyes and entering the void. He searched the void for her, asking her own essence to allow him in. Some days he caught a glimpse of her smiling back or waving at him, but never letting him completely to her.

"You come down every day just to sit under that tree and what, sleep your life away? What are you, fifty? Fifty-one?"

A raspy older voice broke the concentration of the void, bringing Boone back into reality.

They stared at each other for what felt like a full minute before either of them said anything.

"No... What do the young ones call it these days? Meditation? I can't remember what we called it. Meletē perhaps. Which means to practice contemplation." Boone gave himself a little smile.

The old man didn't really care. "Well, I'm missing an opponent. Come over and sit down."

The old man pointed towards an L shape of chairs tucked under tables which had chess boards imprinted onto the top of them.

"It's been a long time since I've played chess." Boone said.

"Good. It'll make it easier to beat you", the old man said without cracking a smile.

Boone shook his head and laughed.

He missed the game and truly enjoyed playing it again. So much so that he added it to his routine every day. Now it wasn't just go to park, enter void, search for Selene, mope on home. It was simply: go to the park, enter the void, search for Selene and then go play chess for the rest of the day.

Every day that passed, he played more chess and searched Selene less. This was okay with Boone. It, in fact, came to a point where he was only searching for her once every week, then once every month.

Mary-Ann and Dunlop could even see that Boone was back to being himself again. Even he himself felt like a new man.

Chapter Thirty

Winter reduced the number of people who were willing to brave the cold and get to the park tables to play chess. This didn't stop Boone, however. He'd lived through much colder years, however maybe in a younger body. Maybe it was the old body he sported now, or maybe it simply was the fact that he was decades old, but Boone thought of himself in a bit of a semi-retirement. He wasn't as active as he once was and second to that, could fall asleep at a moment's notice. It wasn't uncommon for him to fall asleep while waiting for George to come play chess with him.

Boone waited for the old man, George, to come to the park. It was quite a wintry morning, so Boone pulled up his jacket collar over his ears, pulled his head down like a turtle into its shell and tried to keep warm the best he could. The old body he still kept from when he lost Sofija didn't help much. The truth was, Boone knew that he'd be better off healing himself to be back to a young twenty or thirty-year-old. Alas, he did not.

"Good morning." A youthful voice flowed through the air towards Boone.

He was half asleep and heard the repeated words over in his brain as he tried to process them, willing his body to wake.

"Good morning?" The voice said again, this time with a little worry behind it.

Boone looked up in fright. "Oh, good morning!"

A young man was staring at him, barely more than a few metres away. Boone said an unfunny joke about scheduling in his sleep better before moving on and offering him a quick game to which he declined.

The next day, Boone once again sat waiting for his friend George to come join him at the table. He saw the young man out of the corner of his eye approaching the table.

The young man reached out his arm with a burst of nervous confidence. "Phillip Ward", he said.

"Phillip!" Boone said with real confidence. "You're back!"

Boone introduced himself and reached out to shake Phillip's hand. A spark transferred between them before a burst of energy flowed through Boone like he'd never felt before, like a tidal wave of life, death, energy, power and guidance had just crashed down upon him.

He's... a Soul Keeper.

Boone looked up at Phillip, staring into his eyes. He could tell that Phillip differed from the rest, like his soul wasn't just there for himself but for everyone.

They started playing chess and ended up playing until the sun set in the evening. They were instantly like old friends who had some kind of cosmic connection from a past life. He knew who Phillip was, but from Phillip's reaction, he didn't know he was himself yet. He didn't know that his world was about to flip completely upside down.

At the end of the day, they shook hands and promised another game soon. Boone watched as Phillip walked through the gate and out of the gardens.

"He's kind."

Boone jumped at the sudden voice behind him. He turned to see Selene also watching Phillip with a smile.

"Give an old man a heart attack next time." Boone started to pack up the chess pieces from the table.

Selene laughed and put her hand on Boone's back. "You are only as old as you want to be, Boethius."

"Well, I feel old. I've been here too long and look..." He pointed towards the gate which Phillip had just exited. "Looks like I've got another one to guide."

"He is your last."

Boone immediately stood up straight and looked at Selene with wonder. An oddity after all these years.

"My last? Am I dying?" Boone asked, eyes wide open.

"You may if that is what you decide. How old are you, Boethius?" Selene asked.

"I don't remember. It's been so long that I can't even remember what year I was born, let alone the day or month. People didn't care as much back then. I haven't kept track of ninety percent of the time that has passed me by. I'd guess around one thousand nine hundred years."

Selene smiled. "You were born on the 1st of January in the year 19 BCE."

"Wow. I thought I had been born much later. I don't remember it."

"Of course you don't. Do you remember exactly where you were on this date last year? That was only 366 days ago; do you expect to remember anything from two thousand years ago?"

Boone contemplated that thought. "Why are you here now? I've been trying to find you and talk to you for a decade now and you give me nothing."

"You weren't ready and still are not. You need to guide young Phillip through this life first. During this time of guidance, I will show you your own destiny."

"Phillip is important isn't he?" Boone asked.

"Young Phillip Ward will have one of the greatest importance of Soul Keeping over the next two millennia. He will be a master, a guide, just like you were over these last two thousand years. Just like I was a guide to you."

Phillip's training started off a bit differently than Boone was used to doing. He observed how Phillip navigated this world by watching him from a distance. He would always be there if he needed to be, but would never intervene.

Boone recognised Phillip found it difficult to separate his own feelings away from the souls he would take. In one way, this made him more human than any other Soul Keeper; in another way, this hindered his progress.

During this year, Phillip discovered who he truly was. He knew he was a Soul Keeper; he knew he had a path set for him, but he didn't know why. As far as he was aware, he was alone in the world apart from the single appearance by Selene after his friend's death.

It wasn't until the next year that the world really changed for Phillip. A major tragedy fell upon Avondale when a shooter entered a public event and started killing people, one after the other in a horrific event. Boone watched the events unfold until Phillip broke down, begging for help from anyone. Boone sent in Scott to help him as his specialty for soul collection was mass murder, serial deaths and any event which had more than a handful of people. Boone wasn't sure why Phillip was given the eighteen people, but figured it was a test from forces unknown.

This was when Phillip finally found out that Boone was also not just a Soul Keeper, but his guide. He was grilled for hours about who he was, what he knew and what could be next. Boone answered mostly to the best of his ability, but still held back when it came to his personal life.

Boone welcomed the questions, but knew that this was when he had to start training him harder. The next test was Phillip finding Boone in the void.

"How's he doing?" Selene asked.

Selene had been coming to see Boone more often than ever since Phillip's presence made itself known to Boone.

Boone couldn't quite pick why, but he felt like Selene was different now. Like she was more relaxed, more human than he'd ever seen from her in a very long time. To Boone, Selene had spent almost the last two thousand years floating through the world like a ghost or angel. She was there only when she was needed, before disappearing in a poof of clear smoke. He could only suspect that the reason was Phillip being his last student.

"He has a heart. That's good... and bad."

Selene nodded; she knew exactly what Boone meant.

"I've just given him a void test, seeing if he can find me. Shouldn't be too hard, maybe a day or two at the most."

She nodded again. "Well, I have something to show you."

"Such as? We going to get some lunch?" Boone smiled as he asked.

Selene put her head down and a small smile escaped her lips. "No, nothing like that."

"Mhmm, suppose you don't eat."

"Why wouldn't I eat! I'm human, you know!"

"Could have fooled me." Boone said under his breath.

Selene poked him in the ribs as a jest. "Sush, you. I'm going to show you something. So, whenever you're free... we'll... go."

"No time like the present."

Selene once again looked at Boone with a slight look of both annoyance and playfulness. She reached out with her hand palm up, welcoming him to hold on to her hand. He looked at her with a sense of both confusion and wonder about what this could mean. He reached out and held it.

As their hands connected, the world rippled in front of them but only in an area the size of a small tree in an oval shape.

Boone looked at Selene as she squinted her eyes at him. She looked so serious that Boone got slightly concerned about what may be beyond the seemingly transparent ripple. In an instant, the serious expression changed into a full toothy grin and she instantly ran for the ripple, yanking Boone's arm along the way to follow her.

Chapter Thirty One

As they stepped through the ripple, the ground disappeared beneath their feet like they were stepping into thin air. With a momentary lapse in perception, Boone started to tumble around. He caught glimpses of blue as he pinwheeled like he'd just been shoved out of an airplane. They flipped, turned and corkscrewed their way before, in the flash of a light, the ground was there.

With a shocked expression on his face, Boone looked around, trying to establish where the hell he was. He noticed that they were in a completely different location than they had been seconds prior.

"A hospital?" Boone asked.

He looked back towards Selene, a smile still plastered across her face.

"We are in 2011 at the Greenville Hospital. Or at least, just outside of it."

"Right", Boone said. "You can reach into foresight that far? I thought seers only achieved that ability... Are you a seer?"

Lines around Selene's eyes crinkled as she smiled at Boone. He'd never seen that before. Selene to Boone was an entity, a soul herself. She had never been human before, at least in his memory.

"No, I'm not a seer", she continued. "We are actually in 2011 in Greenville."

"What do you mean we're actually in 2011?"

"I meant we were over there." She waved her hand roughly in the direction of Avendale. "Now we are here... in 2011. Our bodies, not our souls."

"We travelled in time?"

Selene shrugged. Such a human-like gesture.

"Why do you keep looking at me all strange-like now?"

"I've never seen you before. This side of you at least", Boone exclaimed.

"You have. When I was your guide a long time ago. Your memory fails you, Boethius."

"So, dare I ask the question?"

"Don't ask me how I can do it; I don't know. Just like when we were Soul Keepers, we didn't know why we were given that ability. You will learn how to do this in time."

"Okay... Next question. Why are we here?"

They looked towards the hospital and a familiar figure started to walk towards the garden they were standing in. Boone looked back and Selene was gone. Not disappeared, but had run behind a nearby tree to hide away from whoever was coming.

Boone walked towards the tree and joined her as they peaked from behind it. As they watched, Phillip Ward walked towards the garden and slumped down in the middle of the grass. Boone looked towards Selene almost as if to ask what he was to do, but she said nothing.

Boone brought himself out from behind the tree and walked slowly over to Phillip who now had his hands on his knees and his eyes closed as he sat on the dry green grass. Boone waited, almost like he didn't want to disturb a quiet dreaming child.

"Hello, Phillip."

Phillip jumped a little and stood up fast. He faced Boone as though he didn't know him at all.

"Now you come! After everything!" Phillip screamed at Boone.

"Woah woah, what is going on? What happened?"

"Dad is dying. He had a heart attack. I need to heal him."

Boone's face dropped and he looked towards Selene who was still hiding. He couldn't see the expression on her face but knew he was here for a reason.

"You can't heal him Phillip, you do not have enough of your own life energy to heal him. You will die. Just wait here. I will heal him. I need to talk to someone first."

Phillip didn't wait; he immediately sprinted back into the hospital, seemingly for his father. Boone stood there in shock as though he wasn't sure what to do now. He wasn't even sure if this was real. He was so used to foresight that these small details didn't immediately bother him.

He turned back towards Selene and jumped at her standing right behind him. He sighed at the sight of her being so close.

"Is Marshall Ward meant to die?" Boone asked.

"Is that what you want?"

"No, why would it be?"

She reached out her hand to him again, the air in front of them once again rippling.

"Then come with me."

The corkscrew ride through the tunnel wasn't any better the second time. They once again landed on grass, but this time it wasn't outside the back of the hospital. This time, they were standing on the back lawn of a cottage at the edge of a lake.

Boone turned towards Selene, waiting for her to answer the unasked question.

"This is the morning Marshall Ward dies."

It was still dark, but Boone looked up to see the sun coming over the horizon. A beam of light cut across the dark morning sky as it rose higher into the air hitting the cottage as Marshall Ward opened his front door.

He stretched and rubbed his chest as he looked over his backyard and down towards the grass. He shook his head slowly before sipping his morning coffee.

Boone could almost see the thought process go through his mind. He, of course, knew that Marshall was about to have a heart attack, so the rubbing of the chest made sense to him. So many deaths over so many years, Boone could tell someone was in trouble before any doctor, nurse or paramedic.

Marshall walked back inside his home momentarily as he slipped his boots over his feet and headed back outside. The rubbing of his chest and arching of his back became more clear as he walked across the grassy yard towards his garden shed.

As though on schedule, Marshall made a small pained 'huugh' sound from his mouth, before he clutched his chest and fell forward.

Boone's eyes grew wider and started frantically looking around to see if anyone was coming to help. He knew he couldn't interfere, but also knew that Marshall had somehow survived this and was going to end up at the hospital.

Time felt like it slowed as they watched over Marshall from a distance. Five minutes passed and still nothing. As far as they could see, Marshall had not moved, nor had his chest risen or fallen in the last four minutes.

A creaking sound came from the neighbour's door as an older man looked out over the grass and saw Marshall face first. The man ran over to Marshall and immediately put his fingers to his neck, checking for a pulse. The man's head fell, then shook.

Boone and Selene remained in the same position, watching over the scene from the outside. They watched as an ambulance parked, rushed to Marshall on the ground and pronounced him dead on the spot.

The look between Boone and Selene told him everything he needed to know.

"You're changing the course of time, aren't you? He's not meant to die and we're here to save him? I don't understand how that is possible."

"Phillip Ward is your student and you are his guide. But you are also his watcher. The outcome of so many souls in this world depends on him saving them. We are not re-writing history, we are not changing history, we are creating the future."

Selene held out her hand before Boone took it once more. They jumped through another ripple in time. This time, they landed in the exact same spot, only moments before.

Boone already knew he had to save Marshall in some way or another. He quickly got up and was about to run. He turned towards Selene.

"How many chances do I have to get this correct?"

"You only need one. You already know you need to save him; whatever you choose is the correct option."

Boone contemplated that for a fraction of a second before running towards the neighbour's house. He knew the old man would be up and looking out the door in roughly five minutes' time, so he needed to speed that up. He picked up a pebble and threw it towards the front door and it made a slight 'tink' sound. He picked up something slightly heavier and it connected with a large single knock.

As the knock on the door rang out, Marshall once again stepped outside his house with his boots on and started to walk across the grassy backyard towards his garden shed. Within seconds, he was flat on his face.

This time, the old man opened his door to the knock, saw Marshall and saved his life.

Chapter Thirty Two

Boone and Selene stepped through their next ripple in time and directly into Mary-Ann.

"What the hell, Boone!" Mary-Ann yelled out. "Where have you been!"

It was 2010, roughly two years since Boone and Selene had left the gardens, travelling through ripples of time watching Phillip. To Boone, however, he'd only seen Mary-Ann a week prior.

Since leaving 2008, Boone and Selene had been watching over Phillip as he traversed the life of a Soul Keeper. Boone saw the frustration in Phillip, not knowing if what he was doing was the right thing. He saw the pain in his eyes as he saved one soul after another after another.

It was an odd feeling to Boone, watching over Phillip from a distance, knowing that the time he was in now wasn't the time he should be in. He was used to foresight, where the choices he made had absolutely no lasting effect.

"I'm Sorry Mary-Ann, I didn't know it had been that long."

"What do you mean you didn't know it had been that long? Are you going crazy, old man? You ending up like Theron?"

Boone's eyelids fell halfway across his eyes as he looked at Mary-Ann sideways, almost like he was saying, 'Really?'.

"No, I'm not turning into Theron. I..." He paused and looked at Selene who gave him a nod.

"I've been watching over Phillip with Selene."

Mary-Ann looked at Selene, a look that was begging for an explanation that Boone couldn't give. Selene shrugged.

Without going into all the details, Boone ran Mary-Ann through everything that had been happening over the last two weeks in his life and what was two years in Mary-Ann's life. If they were all living normal human lives, Mary-Ann would have been calling police, hospitals, even the morgue trying to find Boone. However, an extended period without seeing each other was normal, just not so much these days.

Mary-Ann's life of secrecy was maybe not quite as wild as time travelling through ripples in space, but she knew that not everything was as it seemed. She didn't complain; she didn't worry; she just shook her head.

The next two weeks that followed, Boone and Selene spent more time watching over Phillip as he traversed Soul Keeping. There wasn't a lot that Boone had to step in for, but there were a couple of things that helped along the progress of his training.

Boone watched as Phillip started to not only collect the souls, but talk to them too. One woman, Lisa Lithuana, made a rather large impact on who Phillip was truly going to become.

It wasn't long before time had caught up with both Boone and Selene and they once again found themselves in 2011 outside the hospital where Marshall Ward was now undergoing a major operation on his heart and what started this entire trip to begin with.

The rippling snake pattern dispersed behind them as they stepped through onto the dewy grass of the Greenville Hospital. Boone looked at his watch and tapped the glass.

"Marshall would have had his heart attack a couple of hours ago. It's what... thirty minutes until he's outside trying to find me for the last time."

It wasn't a question. Boone was talking to himself, making sure that he had all the information together.

Boone looked at Selene who gave him a small smile before he walked away towards the hospital. He already knew what he was about to do, just wasn't sure how yet.

He walked up the back steps, entering a small room that served as a second non-emergency entry point to the building. He walked past the reception desk where a woman sat looking at her phone, completely uninterested in the man walking right by her. The signs above him showed the correct way to the intensive care unit, where Marshall would either be undergoing an operation or in one of the hospital beds.

As Boone was half-way to the ICU, he quickly ducked into the building's laundry room where he found a pair of green scrubs and put them on before anyone else walked in. He grabbed a mask on his way out and wrapped it around his face, shielding anyone from seeing that he wasn't actually meant to be there.

The ICU was quiet. It was still early yet, so those who were in there were mostly in from previous days or nights with the odd people such as Marshall, who had found themselves in an unfortunate position so early in the day. Boone was able to see that there was one operating room that had action going on. He picked up a clipboard that was hanging at the front of the room, which read 'Marshall Ward' right at the top.

This was where confidence was key. Boone had to not only act the part of a doctor, but do so with utter confidence that no one would pull him up on being a complete stranger to the hospital. He took a deep breath in, then out and opened the operating room door.

Slow beeps filled the room and quiet chatter went back and forth amongst the doctors and nurses as they worked over Marshall's open chest. No one looked up.

Boone slowly made his way to an open gap where Marshall's head was positioned. One doctor was there, keeping an eye on his heart rate and blood pressure, occasionally telling the doctor what the numbers were every couple of minutes. The doctor looked up at Boone as he positioned himself an arm's length away. They nodded at each other without saying a word.

Before they even had a moment to ask, Boone reached out and laid his hand on the side of Marshall's face. He caressed it like it was his own father, a gentle, warm touch for a body that lay almost dead in front of him.

Energy rushed through Boone's body and entered into Marshall like a flowing tap draining an ever decreasing tank. Fifteen seconds later, Boone removed his hand and walked toward the exit of the operating room.

As soon as he exited into the hallway, he collapsed.

That took more than I realised. I feel weak.

Boone looked around to see if he could see Mary-Ann peaking around the corner waiting for her chance to pounce on his dying body. She wasn't there.

Good, I'd swat her off like a fly. Boone joked to himself.

He gave himself ten minutes to get even a resemblance of energy back into his body. He looked at his watch again, knowing that Phillip was only minutes away from exiting out the back of the hospital.

Picking himself up, he rushed as fast as his body could take him to the back of the hospital. Getting lost along the way, he popped into the room of a patient, planning to swap his scrubs out for something more casual. The last thing he needed was to be seen exiting the hospital like this.

He lifted a pair of brown cargo pants up to his eye line. "Not exactly my style", he muttered to himself as he wriggled them on, followed by a plaid shirt and a cap to shield his old weary eyes.

Exiting the hospital, Boone saw Phillip sitting on the grass once more, his eyes closed and his hands on his knees.

Okay, this is my time to shine. Boone said as he walked towards Phillip.

ॐ

"So... what are you going to do now?" Selene asked Boone.

They both sat on the porch of Boone's home in Avondale. It looked into the surrounding forests of the city. He enjoyed watching nature take its place in his life. He watched as the trees waved their good mornings and the animals danced amongst the bushes in a rotating play every day. Boone, for the life of him, didn't know what he was going to do now.

He shrugged and sipped a beer as he looked out into the trees.

Phillip had mostly finished his initial training by now. Of course, Boone would have to monitor him over time, but he could be mostly trusted to do the correct thing to the right people when needed.

"What will you do?" Boone asked Selene.

It was her turn to shrug. "I have a home in South Caroline, in the USA... In the year 1098... or thereabouts." She said casually.

"Huh..." was all Boone said.

By this time, Boone had gotten a grasp on the inner workings of the ripples, which helped you get from one time to another. Selene had given him a list of rules that he should go by. Not because they had set rules, but because of personal experiences Selene had had from one experience to another.

"How did you..." Boone started to say, but stopped as he looked over and saw Selene was gone. He sighed deeply as he sucked down the last dregs from the bottom of the bottle of beer.

"Okay... Let's try this out." Boone said.

He stood up and looked out one more time towards the forest. Bringing up both of his hands, he closed his eyes and concentrated. He drew an oval shape in the air, trying to create a ripple in front of him almost like he was showing how big of a fish he had just caught. He continued to do this until he heard the squirming ripples come into existence right in front of him. The noise stopped and was replaced with a low and droning 'thump, thump, thump'.

He walked through.

Chapter Thirty Three

The first few steps into this new space were strange. Like someone had just picked him up and dumped him feet first into the middle of a forest. There was no twisting and turning through time like the jumps with Selene previous to this. There were no blurry images that flashed across his eyes. It was a simple thump, step through and he was there.

He looked down at his feet, a pair of flip-flops barely covering them. He lifted one foot to examine it as water dripped off it. The green shrubs of the forest were wet, like a rain had just passed through and the sun had yet to penetrate the thick foliage of leaves, branches and vines.

"Hmm... Northern hemisphere." Boone said to no one.

Taking large steps to avoid the thorny bushes rubbing against his bare leg, he walked towards what looked like a clearing in the forest about two hundred metres ahead.

Boone was used to hearing the morning calls of birds as they tweeted out their greetings to the world. This place, however, had none of that. He could see them in the trees as they watched him step over fallen logs and around anthills. He watched as each bird turned its head sideways, like a confused dog hearing its name for the thousandth time. It was like the birds were also wondering what this man was doing here.

The sunny clearing in the forest was bare, apart from an almost perfectly round cutout from the tree lines creating a grassy green oasis. Boone kept walking until he reached the middle and looked around in each direction. He sucked in a large breath of air and let it out in a long sigh. Clicking out the side of his mouth, he decided he needed to be more prepared than a pair of flip-flops, shorts and a t-shirt one size too small. He brought up his arm once more and started to slowly spin it in the air to create another ripple.

Nothing happened. He tried again, this time with a slight bit more concentration and more 'can-do' attitude. He tried to not think about where he currently was on the planet and allow his mind to open up. Still, nothing happened.

"Huh..." he said, almost like he was stumped on a crossword, rather than stuck in the middle of nowhere and no when.

A crack of a stick rang out through the silent forest. The very sound of something or someone stepping on it. Boone instinctively dropped to the ground, his body laying prone in the long wet grass. Once again, he regretted his fashion choice.

A tweet of a singular bird now echoed across the open field followed by a volley of returning bird songs. The trees and surroundings now sounded like they should with noisy animals and swaying trees.

As Boone still lay unmoving on the ground, he peaked up to see a figure moving across the edge of the forest. It was a man dressed in brown tattered robes, with a rucksack on his back and a machete in one hand cutting a pathway.

Boone squinted his eyes as though he was trying to see who it was. A flash of memory popped into his head. He shook it away. The memory flashed back.

No, it can't be. He said to himself.

He continued to watch the man as he slowly, unwaveringly and confidently trekked across the land until he stopped. Boone peaked atop the grassy knoll at the man, now completely still. They were at a standoff, although one wasn't aware of it.

The man turned towards Boone and looked in his direction, revealing his face. He stayed silent, both not wanting to bring attention to themselves and also not believing what he was actually seeing.

Boone, at a distance, was looking directly into the eyes of himself.

He put his hands to his head trying to even have one memory as to when this might have been. He tapped his temples, punishing himself for not remembering. The flash of memory came back.

"I remember..." he whispered to himself.

It was like déjà vu, but from a different perspective. The time between then and now was vast and it even surprised Boone. Not only because he could remember being there, but because he could remember the feeling of walking through these bushes, feeling the vines rubbing up against his robes. Boone's memory took him back to this time. This memory was good; it was free and joyful. But he dreaded the pain of what was next, knowing that once he reached France, he would be imprisoned and tortured for years.

His heart raced, adrenaline building up in his veins, telling him to stop his past self from making the choices, the choices that put him into the hands of an evil man.

A tear dropped from his eye. He knew that no matter what happened right here and right now; he had to let what was about to happen, happen. Everything from then on has been his path. If he interfered, there would have been so many people in his life that simply would not be. His head dropped, not wanting to see where his past self went as it walked on.

A static sound, almost barely audible, increased to the left of him. Boone looked and saw another ripple hanging in midair. Taking a deep breath, he stood up, banged the dirt off his knees and stepped through the ripple without looking back.

The sound started again; thump, thump, thump, as his body warped through the ripple and he landed again on his feet.

A bell instantly sounded right in his ear as a carriage barely missed him standing in a darkened street.

"Bloody daft cove!" A man yelled from the horse-drawn carriage as it sped away, a fist poking out from the wooden window.

Boone said nothing. He simply stood there, eyes wide, for three seconds before realising where he was. He quickly jumped onto the footpath to get out of the street and out of danger. He looked back up the street, then down. The street was barely visible apart from the light glow of lanterns that were planted every twenty metre gap.

From the aesthetic of the streets, he knew that this was more than likely before 1900 and even more sure that it could have been the early 1800s. His attire definitely would stand out if anyone were to actually catch him in full light, so he was glad for the shadowy city.

The longer Boone stood and looked, the easier it was to narrow down the years. It wasn't a forest like last time and he didn't have an axe, so counting the rings on the trees wasn't valid. He noticed the style of the houses that were built and knocked a few years off his estimate. He walked down the street a little and through a small courtyard and found himself standing outside a partially built Euston Station in London.

"Mid 1837... give or take." Boone said quietly to himself. "Why am I here?"

Boone knew too much about the world of Soul Keepers to know this wasn't just a random coincidence. He sat opposite the station and waited.

It took an hour, but the sun came up and shone across the small buildings of London city. Only minutes after the sun started shining, Boone spotted what he was waiting for. It was once again himself walking down the side of the street, a lunch box in one hand and his other hand tucked into the sleeve of his jacket trying to keep warm.

Boone slowly nodded to himself, knowing exactly where he was going that very morning. Or at least on those mornings.

In 1937 he worked as a maintenance worker and would travel past the Euston Station every day, taking in the progress of the build as it was built larger seemingly every day.

Boone wondered why he was here. Why he was brought into this world again just to see himself once more.

The thumping started again. A ripple opened up next to Boone one more time. He looked around and no one was looking so he stepped on through.

The twirling of traveling was getting easier and this time it felt like he simply stepped through a doorway and was in a completely different world. It only took seconds but what Boone could see completely took his breath away. He knew exactly where and when he was.

Chapter Thirty Four

It had been seventy-five years since this very day. Boone had mostly put it in the back of his mind. He no longer felt anger or the need for revenge. But stepping through now, on this day, at this time, in this place, his nose flared with disgust.

It was the thirteenth of November 1939. The unassuming Foster family were about to be murdered. Boone was not only the one that was about to go down for it, he was almost killed by the actual murderer as well.

Boone knew that he couldn't change the outcome of what had happened to him. But he never actually knew that happened to the actual murderer either. As far as he was aware, this day was always meant to happen. As Selene mentioned, we are not re-writing time; we are creating it.

In this timeline, Boone didn't want to just kick back and watch what was about to happen. He bounced into action and immediately ran to 23 Wrenford Street. He didn't want to waste any time but also knew that if he wasn't careful, he could possibly run into himself. He slowed down a little as he came up to the street.

Looking down at his watch, it didn't help. Time travel didn't automatically adjust his watch for him, so he was out of luck. He simply had to guess what the time was. He hunkered down behind some bushes just opposite the building and waited.

Time was slow, he couldn't get his mind off where he was right now. Just as Boone was thinking about trading up the bush for a nice park bench, he saw his past self walking across the street and into the Wrenford Street flat.

Boone's heart rate went up knowing exactly what was about to happen as he saw the unknown murderer following only thirty seconds behind his past self.

Why was I so careless? Boone thought to himself, slightly shaking his head. I was too comfortable for my own good. Where was my master when I needed him?

He counted in his head. He knew that the murders barely took more than a couple of minutes, so whatever time he had between now and when the man came down the stairs again was all he had.

Boone didn't know what to do; he was at a loss for anything. He couldn't exactly stop him; he couldn't kill him himself as he wasn't that person. But the one thing he knew was that he needed to know why it had happened. Why this man felt like he had to kill this whole family and attempted to kill Boone himself.

He stood up from the bushes like a meerkat looking for enemy combatants. Without a thought, he jogged across the road and stood outside the flat only metres away from the entry point. He was frozen in place, unsure himself what he was doing there.

He heard the loud booted steps of the man racing down the inner stairs of the building, running away from his crimes. He reached the bottom and immediately turned left into the street, almost bumping into Boone.

The man's face fell flat, like he was seeing a ghost for the first time. It was only a few seconds, but felt like it could have been an hour that they were staring at each other. Boone's face was somehow neutral and showed nothing that could give away even a bluff at a poker table.

"Why did you kill me?" Boone asked.

"Uh, uh, uh..." His head swivelled back and forth between Boone and the stairs that led up to the flat.

"I uh..." The man still struggled to speak.

It was like he was a completely different person. The person who stood before him was the same man who had plunged a knife deep into the chest of one Boone before slicing his throat. All with a gleeful grin on his face. That disgusting grin was gone now. What replaced it was a God fearing man. Someone who believed in the afterlife but did not think of it when he was ending the lives of four innocent people.

The man's face went through a flurry of denial, his mind struggling to comprehend exactly what he was seeing. To him, this simply couldn't be true. But it was. Then, in an instant, anger flashed over his face just as fast. He reached his arm back in an arc and swung his fist towards Boone.

Boone knew it was coming; he could see the signs of the clenched fist, the bloodshot eyes and the thousand-yard stare. Yet, Boone didn't move. The man's whole body was shaking from adrenaline, which was shutting down all his bodily functions. He knew that the fist that was coming for him would not connect even in the slightest.

Just as Boone predicted, the man's shaking, wobbly arm flew right past him. The momentum of the arm threw him forward and onto the ground like he was a drunk hooligan on a night out. However, with faster movements and perhaps more flight than fight, he crawled himself to a bench, stood up and ran.

Boone didn't immediately give chase. Not because he didn't want to, but because he didn't need to. This time, the man left behind something of importance. Boone looked down and saw a police badge.

Boone reached down to the ground and picked it up. He looked at it like it was a key to the city. Throwing it up a couple of times, he smiled to himself as he quickly got himself away from the scene before the police would eventually turn up and arrest his past self.

With a few hundred metres between the crime scene and himself, Boone pulled the folded leather square from his pocket. The front of it read 'Police Warrant Card' and had the Royal Coat of Arms emblem above that. He opened it up and saw the name of the murderer clear as day.

"Harold Reginald Whitmore..."

"Whitmore..."

Boone repeated the name over and over in his mouth, just begging for it to mean something. For years he wondered why the man who had tried to kill him was so adamant not only about killing the family, but ensuring Boone lasted long enough to then come back and kill him, or at least he thought he did.

He didn't know what to feel. On one hand, he was finally able to speak the name of the man who ruined this part of his life. On the other hand, he still couldn't see the reason behind it. Boone wasn't sure who he could go to now. He couldn't exactly go and ask Dunlop who this guy might be... or could he?

Before long, Boone found himself standing on the steps of the London Metro Police Station. The extensive building looked small compared to what it had looked a lifetime ago when he was in handcuffs. Now, there were no feelings behind it.

Walking up the stairs, he knew that his past self would also be in this building by now. However, that would be from the back of the building and the infamous face of the Wrenford Street killer would yet to be known throughout the city.

Inside the station, it was a bustling scene of both uniformed police and civilians reporting thefts, accidents or concern over an upcoming war. Boone stood at the back of a line that slowly got shorter and shorter as time went on, eventually making it to the front.

"Hi, I need to speak with Detective James Dunlop."

The reception policeman stood up slightly and looked down and then back up at Boone, taking in both his demeanor and what he was wearing. He ticked his mouth slowly, imagining what the world had come to, walking into a police station like he's just gotten out of bed.

"Detective Dunlop is very busy right now! That would be impossible. If you have something to report, I can take in the notes and hand them directly to our team."

Boone cleared his throat. "That won't do. I need to see Detective Dunlop..." There was a silent standoff between them both, "Please tell him that Boone is here."

A quick sound came from the mouth of the officer, one that sounded an alarm of annoyance. Nevertheless, he got up and walked out the back.

Silence ensured before a loud "What!... what do you mean he is out the front?"

Dunlop burst through the door to the front reception desk and looked directly at Boone. His eyes grew wide, unsure of what he was truly seeing. He scampered around the desk and grabbed onto Boone's arm, dragging him into the first room he could get him into.

"We've lived a long time, mate and it's hard to say that either of us are surprised at anything that goes on now. But mate, you've got one over on me. I just saw you out the back! Albeit, you were slightly younger and... not dressed... like this." Dunlop waved a hand all over in a flurry.

"I know. It's difficult to explain fully. I'm aware of what is happening out the back of the station right now. It's going to be difficult for him, so you need to be there as much as you can. You can't do much, but you can be there at the end."

Boone carried on, "Look... I'm from the future. I can't tell you how or why I'm here, but I need one answer from you, then I'm leaving."

Boone handed the warrant card to Dunlop who easily took it. If there were questions Dunlop wanted to ask, he didn't; he simply believed what was being told to him by his oldest friend and accepted it for what it was.

"Where did you get this?" Dunlop asked.

"He was the one who killed the family on Wrenford Street. Almost killed me at the same time."

Dunlop was shocked. Not at the idea of Boone not being the killer, he already knew he'd never do that. But at the idea of it being someone from the police force.

"This is Sergeant Whitmore. Aged thirty-eight, he joined the force just like his old man and his father before him. He's untouchable and a right twat. Do you need help?"

"No, I just need to know where to find him."

Ten minutes later, Boone was back on the outside of the station, walking away. He didn't know exactly what he was about to do, but he knew where he was going.

The police station was right on the Thames and Boone needed to head north towards Soho where Harold Whitmore lived. It took him an hour to walk towards Rathbone Street, but that gave him time to think about what he might do or say. Or at least that's what he had hoped. The truth of it was, he simply had no idea, yet here he was.

Boone knocked three times on Harold's red front door.

Chapter Thirty Five

"Yes?" A woman stared straight at Boone from inside the home of Harold. An unexpected twist to who would seem a psychopathic killer.

A wife? Friend? Neighbour? Boone thought to himself. The seconds ticking down awkwardly filled with nothing but silence.

The woman dried her hands on her apron as she still stared at Boone. A friendly smile came to her face as she tilted it, confused.

"Sorry, Ma'am." Boone rubbed his forehead. "I am Sergeant O'Dowd. Is Mr Whitmore in?"

"Oh! Yes, of course, please do come in. He's just in his den, I'll go fetch him." The woman said with surprising nicety.

Boone walked into the house. A clean, simplistic styled family home. A green three-person sofa sat centred in the family room with blankets wrapped over the top. Pictures of Harold smiling alongside what Boone guessed was his wife and two small children, a boy and girl. He sniffed in the amazing aroma of freshly baked bread, which wafted in from the kitchen next door. It was the house of a family man.

Boone's back was turned away from Harold as he walked in. "Well, hello there!" a cheery voice came from behind before he turned and faced the murderer.

As though in slow motion, the face of a happy, cheery, loving family man turned horrid as he recognised the face of the man he not only thought to have killed, but then had been arrested. The snarling face was filled with both confusion, rage and bloodlust.

Harold reached for a fire poker, which was within arm's length away from him and ran towards Boone. With it lifted above his head, he swung down. Boone anticipated the swing and dodged to his right as the poker clanged against a metal rack of family photos. The poker lifted again, this time swinging left and right and side to side as Harold swung for Boone, attempting to hit at least something. Running out of space, Boone jumped over the couch and attempted to move as far from danger as he could. The sharp end of the poker connected with his face, cutting Boone from his jaw to his upper cheek.

"Harold! What are you doing!" his wife screamed from the kitchen, her face a picture of frightened, pained confusion.

"Shut up, bitch!" He screamed back at her, pointing the poker at her now. "You! This is your fault!"

He rushed towards her, mirroring his swing he made at Boone. She wasn't as lucky as it connected with the top of her skull, knocking her to the ground and out cold. Boone knew she wasn't dead. There wasn't any sign of that or any Soul Keepers nearby.

Harold turned back towards Boone who was holding his face, keeping the blood from seeping out. He ran back towards him, but this time dropping the poker and leading with his fists. He swung and connected again with the left side of Boone's face. Now, Boone was on somewhat of an even playing field. He knew hand to hand combat and had been taught by many people over many years.

Boone retaliated. Without a second thought after his own hit, he leveraged his whole body around from the right side and, using the momentum of his other arm twisting left; he brought his elbow up and connected forcefully with Harold's nose. His head went back like a light bulb just turning off. Bloody spurted from his nose as he stumbled back, his brain trying to not to fade into unconsciousness. Unluckily, he regained his composure and lifted his fists into the air like a backyard boxer, half covering his face from any potential blows.

It was Boone's turn to rush. He ran for Harold, faked right, went left and swept his leg under him, sending him tumbling sideways to the ground. Without letting him get his bearings, Boone wrapped his legs around Harold's throat and squeezed. Thirty seconds later, his body went limp. It didn't kill him; Boone wouldn't have done that, but he was out of danger for now.

He quickly got up off the ground and rushed towards Harold's wife on the ground. She was moaning as she lay. Boone came up behind her and lifted her head slightly, placing a towel under it. He took another one and pressed it gently onto the open wound on her head.

She moaned again, moving her lips trying to talk. Boone waited, unsure of how much time he would really have. He looked back and saw the chest of Harold rise and fall, a clear sign that his breathing was normal and not in any risk himself.

"Is he dead?" He heard her ask weakly.

"No, your husband is fine."

The woman started to whimper. "Why... please", teardrops fell from her eyes as she begged, "Please, kill him, save me."

Boone moved the hair away from her face, trying to comfort her the best he could. He looked up towards Harold and he was gone. Boone looked around in a panic, trying to see or hear where he had gone.

Three seconds later, Harold appeared at the kitchen door. He held a revolver in his hand and had it pointed at Boone from less than three metres away.

"You... I don't know how you are doing this. You should be... dead, arrested, I don't know! But now, I'm going to make sure you're dead for sure this time!"

Boone closed his eyes and his life flashed before them. A mostly happy life, people who he loved, people who loved him. The jobs he held and the people he helped. The souls he saved and the people who he helped become Soul Keepers themselves. He thought about Mary-Ann and Phillip, silently apologising to them for just leaving them and not telling them where he was going.

They'll never know; they'll always wonder why I ran away and where I went.

I'm sorry, I love you.

The loud explosion of a bullet exiting the chamber of a gun rang out through the room, followed by the sound of it entering a body. Boone shut his eyes even tighter, wondering when the burning pain of being shot would start.

It didn't. Boone opened his eyes just in time to see the body of Harold Whitmore fall to the ground with a thud. Behind Harold was an old man, hands shaking, holding a revolver himself pointed towards where Harold used to be. He lowered the weapon, still shaking.

"I always hated that bastard as a neighbour." The old man said.

೩๏

From Boone's perspective, it had been almost eight decades, but he finally got both his answer and revenge. From Harold's perspective, it took him less than a day to have his life changed.

Harold didn't die that day. In fact, he lived for another forty years after it. However, his life was never the same. When he was shot by his neighbour, the bullet entered his head and connected with his brain. It damaged vital cognitive sections and caused severe brain damage.

He lived in a hospital for the rest of his life, mostly laying in the same bed or chair, watching the same room and listening to the same beeps on the machines as his day ticked on, day after day. The doctors and nurses said he couldn't even think for himself, even if he tried. Boone would argue that fact. He spent several jumps through the ripples, going to see Harold as he withered away lonely in the hospital. Every time he visited, Boone could see the terror in Harold's eyes as he realised time and time again who was coming to visit him.

There was a part of Boone that felt sorry for him. He believed he should have been locked away in prison for the rest of his life, but not this. The prison in his head may have been too far. He guessed that either death or whatever this was, would have been the only option. It would have been impossible for him to go to prison for the actual murders of the foster family, as Boone had already been accused of those for decades.

Harold Whitmore was a terrible man to everyone he met. He was abusive and abrasive. He manipulated people and charged others with crimes they did not do. He hit and hurt his wife and children every day of their lives. Their wonderful home was only wonderful due to the terror which his wife, Ann, faced every day, feeling that if she made one wrong move, he would kill her.

As it turned out, the reason he went and killed the Foster family was because Harold thought that his wife was having an affair with John Foster. The truth, however, was that she was tutoring both of the Foster children in private piano lessons for extra money. Harold's rage for John turned into blood shed which no one apart from his own scared family could see coming.

Even though Harold did not face prison time. The day he decided to murder the Foster family was his last day as a free man.

As for why he targeted Boone? There was no reason. He was at the wrong place at the wrong time.

Chapter Thirty Six

A rippled wave closed behind Boone as he stepped back through into the year 2015 and onto his back porch. He'd not made it back perfectly to the same time he left, but it was pretty close. He dusted himself off, picked up the glass beer bottle that was sitting on the arm of his bench chair and walked in the back door of his home.

"Hey, where have you been?" Mary-Ann asked out of a full mouth, throwing another cube of cheese into it.

Boone smiled at her, remembering all the good times they had together.

"Ah, nowhere. Was just finishing something that someone else started." He pointed towards the backyard.

Mary-Ann laughed. "Okay, well, everyone is coming over, remember and don't tell me you forgot!" she said, waving at his shorts and flip-flops.

Laughing, Boone said, "No, I remember. I'll go put some pants on."

He walked to his room, took a shower, shaved, put on some clean pants and a shirt and walked back out to the living room.

Boone looked around the room, smiling to himself about how lucky he was to have all of these people. Mary-Ann laughed as she and Mel Ward whispered to each other. Phillip, Adam and Summer huddled around each other reminiscing about the old high school days. Scott lazed out on the couch, a beer in one hand, his phone in the other. Dunlop and Maggie slow danced in the kitchen. This was his family, everyone he loved.

A hand fell upon Boone's shoulder as he sipped his own drink. He looked to see Selene standing next to him.

"I trust you found what you were looking for." She asked.

"I did."

Authors Notes

Thank you once again for giving my Soul Keeper series a go. If you've read this far, that means you've gotten through the journey with Boone and learnt about a small fraction of his life.

I found this book a lot more challenging than Phillip's story. You probably can't call this book a prequel or sequel to the first, but more of a spin-off. I immediately had Boone's journey in my mind as I was writing Phillip's story; I just didn't know exactly what would happen after that first court scene. It was hard because I wasn't used to writing true historical events woven into my storyline. I wanted to give Boone's life a proper fantasy but at the same time I wanted it to ensure I wasn't screwing up Earth's proper timeline. I think I did a pretty good job of that. If you follow the path that Boone took out of the prison, you can follow his steps on a map, street for street. The buildings that were mentioned and the people that existed should have been perfectly true. This goes for a lot of the story.

If you're someone who knows me, you may recognise some names or descriptions of some people along the way. I think I saw Boone as a bit of myself, although he's always been much older in my mind – perhaps more in line with what Phillip saw and more than likely around the age of my own dad. When Mary-Ann appeared, my brain immediately told me that this was my daughter. I was protective of her in the same way I am of Eliza, my real daughter. You'll see Stuart Adam in the book and find my brother Stuart. It's true, he's slightly taller than me, slim and has the trademark eye creases that he gets from my dad.

I also wrote into the book a storyline of James, a firefighter in Liverpool who died during the blitz. This is actually a great-uncle of mine who I share two names. I tried to have as many details about him as accurate as I could. From his uniform to the street he died on and the way he died. I hope I did the right thing by him.

I find writing odd in a way. I wrote the book over the course of three months and thought I was going to have to re-write more than two-thirds of the whole story. It wasn't until I started editing and reading through it that I found I really loved the story that I wrote for Boone.

So, what will you see next? I'm not sure. My intention from the beginning of this book was to write about Mary-Ann. I didn't know it at the time, but she showed herself when Boone was lost. I think he needed her in his life just as much as she needed him. We know a bit of her story and who she is. But even you as the reader and myself as the writer don't yet know what Mary-Ann faced as a child, or anything about the decade long training that Theron put her through. She has a mysterious life and we almost know nothing about her being an actual Soul Keeper. So, I guess I'm saying that I don't know yet.

In the meantime, I'm hoping to write some short stories and put those out as eBooks. We'll see how that turns out.

I thank you again for reading my stories. It truly means a lot to me that so many people have read and commented in such a positive way. You mean the world to me.